T5-CVC-298

Susy's
Scoundrel

Susy's Scoundrel

By Harold Keith

Illustrations by John Schoenherr

THOMAS Y. CROWELL COMPANY
NEW YORK

Copyright © 1974 by Harold Keith

All rights reserved. Except for use in a review, the reproduction or utilization of this work in any form or by any electronic, mechanical, or other means, now known or hereafter invented, including xerography, photocopying, and recording, and in any information storage and retrieval system is forbidden without the written permission of the publisher. Published simultaneously in Canada by Fitzhenry & Whiteside Limited, Toronto.

Designed by Angela Foote

Manufactured in the United States of America

Library of Congress Cataloging in Publication Data

Keith, Harold, date
Susy's scoundrel.

SUMMARY: An Amish girl in Oklahoma adopts two coyote pups, but their mother steals them back and their subsequent activities put them in deadly peril.
[1.   Coyotes—Fiction]   I.   Title.
PZ10.3.K248Su   [Fic]   74-1052
ISBN 0-690-00496-6

1 2 3 4 5 6 7 8 9 10

for my grandson
CASEY JOHN KEITH

BY THE AUTHOR:

The Bluejay Boarders
Brief Garland
Komantcia
Rifles for Watie
Sports and Games
Susy's Scoundrel

Contents

Susy's
Scoundrel

If Susy Zook, a little Amish girl, had not wanted a coyote for a pet, this story would never have happened.

A shy creature of eight, Susy had an affinity for animals, moving easily and unafraid among the heavy draft horses that had pulled her father's plow.

If Peter, her father, had stayed with those horses instead of buying the tractor, he wouldn't have had the dispute with his church that brought down all the trouble on the Zooks.

I

Susy's parents belonged to the Plain People, as the strictest Amish called themselves. They fastened their clothing with hooks and eyes instead of the more worldly buttons. A peaceful folk, they opposed war and believed in non-resistance. They regarded the devil as a relentless foe whom they sought to defeat by following the New Testament word for word and by rejecting such modernisms as automobiles, electricity, telephones, motion pictures, steam heat, radios, and tractors. But their honesty and thrift were unquestioned and, despite their quaint ways, they were often better farmers than their neighbors.

Defiantly, Peter had purchased the tractor. With it, he could cultivate his Pennsylvania soil more quickly and efficiently than by using horses. He was resolved to adopt those of the new ways that made the land more productive. He was convinced that this did not violate the Amish precept that God placed man on earth to love his neighbors, till the soil, and to obey the principle that life on the land is the only right life for man.

As Peter knew that he would, he soon got a disapproving visit from Jacob Yoder, the Amish bishop. And when Peter continued to use his tractor openly, the bishop expelled him from the church, thus placing Peter's soul in eternal jeopardy.

"We didn't excommunicate you," the bishop told him; "you excommunicated yourself."

For five weeks, Peter Zook was shunned by his Amish neighbors. They would visit hospitably with his wife but walk away when he came up. His wife was forbidden to sleep in the same bed with him; neither could she nor Susy dine with him at the same table. In spite of that, he kept the tractor, coating all its lamps with black paint to prevent pridefulness.

Finally, Peter knew that he was facing an unresolved conflict. He sold his Pennsylvania farm. Traveling with his family half way across the nation, he started over again in western Oklahoma.

There Susy grew up on her father's farm near the Wilderness, a cactus-fringed expanse of mesquite and varmints and rattlesnakes that was rich in off-beat beauty. There scores of coyotes would die in the shadow of one red ridge because of the lamb-killing sins of one of their number whom the others seldom saw.

And that's what this story is about, too.

Susy Zook

On a late afternoon in April, when the sun's beams were firing the buttes and shadowing the arroyos, Susy got her coyote, and lost him, all within the space of an hour.

With a bucket of soapsuds and a broom, the girl was helping her mother wash down the outside of the house when George Boston, a neighbor, walked up. He was carrying a shovel. With him was Gilbert, his son, who went to the White Bead school with Susy. All around them frolicked the Boston hounds, mild eyed, wavy tailed, their long noses sniffing at everything in the yard.

"Howdy, Miz Zook," said George Boston. "Can Susy go with us? We're gonna reset a fence post and exercise the hounds a little. We're walking. Be back in an hour or so."

"For her, that would be *plesseerlich*," said Rebecca. Eyes shining, Susy accompanied them with long, eager strides, one hand stroking a hound's head.

In a badger hole at the edge of the Wilderness, the dogs found a den. With the spade he had brought, George Boston dug out six squirming coyote babies, each woolly, short muzzled, and cinnamon furred.

With a gasp of pleasure, Susy pounced upon one, a male whose coat shone more coppery than that of any of the others.

"*Ach!*" she cried. "How pretty it is!" Delighted by the fulfillment of her dearest desire, she cuddled him fondly to her heart, caressing him and admiring him.

The coyote mother, peering from behind a sage brush, had witnessed the abduction of one of her brood. Torn with fear and anguish, she acted quickly and courageously to recover him and lure the strangers away from the others.

When she barked from a nearby hill, then showed herself, the dogs went after her. George Boston and both children followed, running and walking behind the hounds.

Susy, wearing the Amish long stockings, poke bonnet and skirt that reached to her shoe tops, was running with her pup in her arms. It became heavy. Soon the girl was panting with fatigue.

"Why don't you leave him here?" George Boston suggested, pointing to a depression under a sage clump. "He won't run off. He hasn't even got his eyes open yet. We'll get him when we come back."

Reluctantly, Susy laid the pup in the hole. For nearly an hour they continued following the hounds. That was exactly what the coyote mother wanted them to do. Two years old, she had boundless imagination and had learned a lot. The older a coyote gets, the wiser it becomes.

When the party returned to the hole, tired and sweaty, the coppery pup was gone. They had not gone half a mile from it before the mother, eluding the dogs, had circled back, snatched it up, and got away.

Susy stood stiffly, the back of one hand tight to her lips to hold back a sob.

And when they hurried to the spaded-out den to retrieve another pup for her, they found that the mother had also been there. One at a time by the scruff of their necks, she had moved all six babies to another burrow and at that same moment was licking them and loving them as they nursed at her breast.

"Oh," moaned Susy, "they're gone too." Her brown eyes enormous with despair, she lifted her apron, burying her face in it and whimpering broken-heartedly.

Two weeks later, Susy got the coppery one back. It was a matter of rare good luck for both the girl and the coyote. Peter Zook had lost a cow that morning. Hunting for the lost animal, Peter had ridden up behind Jud Bodkins, the wolfer, who had found a new den that the same coyote mother had dug in a sandbank near a creek.

Greedy and dirty and uncouth was Jud Bodkins with a whiskery face as merciless as the steel traps he set about the Wilderness. He was not a salaried hunter; consequently he had no interest in the war against coyotes that was being pushed by the farmers and ranchers trying to save their sheep. But the court clerk at Huckel paid a two-dollar bounty for each pair of coyote ears anybody brought in, even those of the coyote pups.

So Jud looked first for dens, knowing that coyote babies abounded in them in April. Their scalps would buy the whisky he so loved to guzzle, as well as cartridges for his rifle and liver for his traps.

When Peter Zook rode up, Jud Bodkins was on his knees beside the new den he had freshly spaded out. Four little coyote corpses lay in a row on the sand, victims of the ball-peen hammer in his hand.

Thrusting his left arm into the den, the wolfer pulled out the last two whelps. He dropped one of them and reached for his hammer. The coppery-furred pup he held blinked helplessly in the sunshine, bright-eyed and trembling, missing its mother's warm breast and tender manner. It was the same one Susy had previously carried and lost. This fact, of course, nobody knew.

"Man, stop awhile now," Peter Zook called in his soft deliberate voice.

Jud Bodkins whirled around. He saw a tall, straight-backed stranger sitting a buckskin horse. The stranger's dark coat had neither collar nor lapels nor outside pockets. Beneath the broad-brimmed hat that sat squarely on his head, his hair was banged straight across his forehead, like a schoolgirl's. He wore a full beard but his upper lip and cheeks were cleanly shaven.

"How would you price that one?" asked Peter Zook. "I'll give you something for him." His face, round as a drum and sunburned the color of walnut, was calm and affable. To Jud Bodkins, he looked like a traveling preacher of some odd religious sect.

Jud lurched to his feet, still clutching the coyote pup. Its reddish fur seemed to pick up some of the sunlight, blending with the color of the surrounding soil.

"Why you want him?" he demanded, eyes narrowing suspiciously. He had not heard the buckskin approach and seemed to resent being surprised.

"My little girl wants him for to play with," Peter Zook answered politely. The buckskin had shied when the wolfer stood, snorting through its nose, but Peter

Zook's sinewy hands tightened on the reins, controlling the animal.

"Where you live?" persisted the wolfer, curtly.

With a long arm, Peter Zook gestured half a mile behind him to what he had built in four years.

A new frame house, neatly whitewashed, with Dutch shutters and gates painted blue stood on a small eminence near the county highway to White Bead. Everything looked stitched together like squares on a quilt. There was a red barn, trees planted in lanes, fields patterned in arrow-straight rows. An orchard of apple, peach, and apricot flanked the house, bounded by a mulberry hedge trimmed low and flat on top. Unmarked by power poles or TV antennas, the scene was pleasantly unfamiliar and picturesque.

"Who you work fer? Who owns thet house an' land?"

"They're mine, mister," said Peter Zook, quietly. His modesty was lost upon Jud Bodkins who had just moved to the Wilderness country and did not know that Peter Zook had learned soil enrichment, crop rotation, and animal husbandry from Amish forebears who had been practicing it long before there were county agricultural agents in the land. One of the secrets of Peter's success was that he arose early enough in the morning to plow the dew under and did not stop plowing until the dew fell again at evening.

Jud Bodkins glared as him sourly. "Gimme two

dollars an' you kin have him," he growled, "That's what the county pays. Save me havin' to brain him and cut off his ears."

And that's how Susy Zook recovered her coyote. Subtracting two one-dollar bills from his leather purse, her father bought it from the wolfer.

He also purchased its brother, unwilling to see it slaughtered either. Half an hour later he came riding up to the back door of his home with both pups cowering in his saddlebag, lonely, frightened, and understanding nothing. And from the top of the knoll behind him, the coyote mother watched, her yellow eyes inscrutable.

Standing barefoot in a kitchen chair while Rebecca, her mother, braided her hair at the back of her neck, Susy was saddened by her father's telling of the fate of the other four pups. She asked Rebecca the age-old question: Why had they died?

"God called them," answered the mother. "They passed on to Heaven."

That night, Susy slipped outdoors to ponder that. Tilting back her head, she looked at the stars crackling in the Oklahoma sky and whispered earnestly, "God, don't call that red one for awhile. You don't need him."

For a month and a half, Susy Zook and the coyote mother fought a classic duel for possession of those two pups. Susy had learned from her previous loss how clever and determined coyote mothers can be.

What she did not know was that these were the first pups that mother had ever birthed.

Because of the massacre of the other four by Jud Bodkins, she longed for these remaining two all the more and thought of nothing except how she might recover them from the human beings she feared and distrusted.

At first, Susy herself became a mother. Several times each day, she fed the stub-nosed pups warmed cow's milk from a nippled bottle and laughed with delight at how noisily and enthusiastically they suckled it. To her, they were charming little puffballs of fluffy innocence and she loved to caress their fur, soft and silky as a kitten's, and to look into their blank, blue eyes.

Rebecca, her own mother, big, strong and buxom, was constantly warning her daughter of the day both coyote pups would return to the wild.

"The wolf you may feed as much as you like, but he will always glance toward the forest," she reminded Susy. But Susy closed her ears to that discouraging maxim and busied herself living in the present. And the coyote babies thrived.

Their hunger knew no bounds. With the girl cradling them in her arms, and feeding them before and after school, they grew as rapidly as the sweet clover yellowing along the fence lines. Reddy soon learned his

name and that when Susy whistled to him, it usually meant food. From milk they progressed to rabbits that Peter Zook slew for them with his shotgun.

Susy was the only person from whom the pups would accept food. When Peter Zook gave the first rabbit carcass to Susy, who in turn gave it to the coyote pups, he said, "Daggone rabbits been stuffing themselves on my young wheat and something else my green maize heads has been eating. A hundred coyotes I wish I had to keep all the diehinker pests thinned out. I'd save money."

That night, Susy discovered that the young coyotes had not left anything of the rabbit. Mystified, she asked her father about it.

"Coyotes like hair with their meat, I guess," he replied. "They'd probably starve to death if red beef-steak was all they had to eat."

At first, the pups backed up in fright from everything they did not understand. A sudden noise, like the sliding across the floor of Peter Zook's chair when he pushed it back from the dinner table, startled them. Their memories were indelible.

If a footstool was out of place in a room from one day to the next, they shrank back and viewed it with as much perplexity as they would have a tree out of place in the wild. Even in puppyhood, there was a quickness and wildness about them that contrasted strangely with the dog pups on the premises.

They hated cats and rushed every one they saw, compelling them to climb trees, porch posts, or whatever surface was available. Dogs they did not fear. They always went right up to them and wanted to play.

Susy learned that she must never put her hands on them too quickly. Reddy rarely let her touch him with her left hand. Her right hand was the one with which she fed him; in it he had full confidence.

Neither coyote wanted to be touched while eating. When she did touch them under those circumstances, they would cringe, dodge back, and look at her with a strange glint of barbarism in their round eyes, which were beginning to turn pale yellow.

The other pup, which had ash-colored fur, would bury the food he could not eat. Soon he learned to stand on his hind legs, front feet dangling limply, and beg for apples. Unlike the dogs on the place, he enjoyed the baths Susy gave him in the tank beneath the windmill, whining with pleasure.

He soon learned to fetch the stick she threw and lay it at her feet. But when she stooped to pick it up, he would sometimes snatch it quick as lightning, back up a step, and dropping it again, dare her to try to beat him to it.

"You're *nixnootzach*," she told him, shaking her head. Because of his mischievous nature, she called him Skeezix.

Reddy was the first to learn to hunt. When he

heard the rustling of a mouse in the weeds, he would stop suddenly, cock his ears, and listen. Then he would leap into the air in a sky hop, and come down on the rodent with his front paws. Grasping it in his mouth, he would throw it back playfully over his shoulder and catch it before it dropped. Finally, he would eat it.

Fear, bred in his bones, always showed when he heard a sudden noise or saw an unfamiliar object. A squeak of the windmill, or the shadow of its wheel and vane moving across the lawn when the wind swung it around, panicked him so greatly that he would run into his box in the hay shed and hide.

When Rebecca, brandishing a broom, would drive him from her parlor when she caught him chewing a wolf skin rug there, Reddy would run to Susy and hide beneath her long skirt. However, she soon forbade him this harbor of refuge when he began to nip her ankles in play.

Once when Susy, with soap and lye water, was scrubbing the back porch of native sandstone, a railroad streamliner's air horn moaned from the distance, its sound curiously flawed by the wind.

To Susy's amazement, Reddy sank back on his haunches, raised his muzzle, and began to howl in a manner so unspeakably mournful that the girl felt strangely moved.

Starting with a series of sharp, staccato yips that became faster and higher pitched, the young coyote's

wailing ended in a long, quavering squawl that died
away in smothered yaps and gurgles, plunging all the
dogs on the place into an imitative uproar. Hearing it
from close range for the first time, Susy thought it the
wildest, saddest, most beautiful music that she had ever
listened to.

On the following Sunday morning, she heard it
again. The day dawned beautiful but Susy was not
surprised. She knew that it would be beautiful because
the night before the cows had come home with their
tails down instead of straight out behind them. That
always brought a pretty day, her German grandmother
had told her.

Like her grandmother, Susy believed that super-
stitions were the shadows of great truths. She believed
that when you rode over a railroad track, you should
raise your feet and cross your fingers to avoid bad
luck. Apples picked when the horns of the moon
tilted up were juicier and made better *lodwarrick,*
apple butter. You should always stir cake dough
clockwise or the cake would fall. A child stepped over
would not grow or thrive; step back over it quickly.

The Zooks were seated in the Methodist church
at White Bead, which they now attended since there
was no Amish house of worship nearby. Peter wore a
fresher version of his somber attire, homemade broad-
fall trousers of twill, gray denim shirt with no necktie,
black tail coat fastened with hooks and eyes, and

high-top shoes. Beneath Rebecca's white prayer cap, her flaxen hair was parted in the middle and closely combed down toward the temples. Her brown dress, full and wide, was made with a cape over the shoulders and an apron fastened over it. Susy was dressed exactly as her mother. Straight pins, rather than buttons, held their dresses together. Neither wore jewelry nor makeup.

After the sermon, the choir sang a closing hymn. As the last strain died away, a discordant cry burst from outside the building.

At first, it sounded like a dog. But the barking of a dog is monotonous because a dog repeats his phrasing and his tone. This was wild, stirring music that belonged to the prairies and the buttes. The musician yapped with constantly changing intonations, the short high-pitched notes rising over one another shrilly and ending in a melancholy scream.

Surprised and hushed by this eerie contribution to the harmony of the choir, the congregation stirred uneasily, then began to smile and whisper to each other.

In the pew between her parents, Susy Zook clapped her hand over her mouth. It sounded like her Reddy.

It was her Reddy, they discovered later when they left the church and climbed into Peter Zook's black buggy. The coyote pup emerged from the tall roadside grass, his mouth agape in a wide grin. He was obviously glad to see them.

"Lookie there," said Peter Zook, pointing with his finger. "The snap on his collar. He accidently opened it. He must have been trying to chew it off, yet."

All the way home, Susy sat on her knees in the buggy seat with her back to the horse. Through the rear curtain, raised for ventilation, she watched Reddy loping along in the adjacent field. She was glad he had followed them instead of trying to join his mother in the wild. She hoped the mother had forgotten him.

But the love of a coyote mother is deep and enduring. Next day, the Zooks walked to their pasture garden to gather vegetables, taking along both pups. Halting beneath a hackberry tree, they began eating the lunch they had brought in a paper sack. Peter tossed half an apple each to Reddy and Skeezix. Both pups began devouring them.

Suddenly a coyote barked from the nearby sage. Reddy and Skeezix raised their heads curiously, then resumed eating.

Peter, who had been lying down, rolled to his knees, staring in the direction of the sound.

"The mother coyote. That's her, I'll bet a nickel," he said.

Susy sat up, huddling herself into a shivering knot of fear. "What she want?"

"She maybe want us run out in the sage and chase

her so she can run around behind us and get her pups back again. She knows a gun I haven't got or she wouldn't come this close."

"How does she know that?" panted Susy, biting down on her trembling lip.

"She can see that I haven't. Her nose maybe told her so, too. Burned powder from an uncleaned gun, they know what it smells like. They know what a fresh oiled gun smells like, too. Dogs, guns, men—they can smell them a quarter mile off, especially when there's a little wind."

Susy leaped to her feet and whistled. "Reddy! Skeezix! Come here!" Reddy picked up the remainder of his apple and came obediently. Skeezix gulped the rest of his and followed more leisurely.

All the way home, the girl worried about it. "I'm not going to let her have them," she told herself firmly. "They're mine, now."

Next day, Peter made leashes for the coyotes by snapping a rope to the metal ring of a leather collar for each. That night, Susy not only locked them in the shed, but made doubly sure of their security by tying them to the wheel of a plow.

"I'm your mama now," she told them. "Forget about that other one."

But the other mother did not forget about them.

The Chewed Collar

Rain, preceded by hail, lashed the land that night but Susy, alone in bed, was not frightened. Her grandmother had told her that the thunder was "the moving of God's feet along the sky," and that the lightning was "the winking of His eye." Something else she found next morning disturbed her more.

What she found was the coyote mother's tracks all around the shed where the pups were confined. And she found something else, too.

Near the door, the mother had dug a shallow hole. In it, slightly covered with the damp earth, lay what looked like a mass of red meat, fresh and undigested. Puzzled, Susy called her father.

"Chewed rabbit meat, it looks like," said Peter Zook. "She's so crazy about her pups that she's afraid we're not giving them enough food. So she's trying to feed them herself."

"How papa?" asked Susy. "They're in the shed. She's outside."

"By killing the meat and swallowing it in chunks, then coming here and throwing it up into this hole she dug. The pups, she knows, will smell it. They will dig it up, she hopes, and eat it when we let them out."

With the toe of his boot, he raked off the fresh earth, disclosing more of the meat. "I think it will be all right to let them eat this," he said. "Fresh it looks. I'll bet you she killed the rabbit this morning and carried it two, three miles. Easier to carry it in her stomach than in her mouth."

Going to the barn for a shovel, he carefully scooped up the regurgitated food and Susy carried it inside the shed. The coyote pups quickly began to devour it.

"They eat lot more than a dog their size," Peter said, leaning thoughtfully against a stanchion, "maybe more rabbits I should shoot."

All morning Susy fretted over the coyote mother's

determination. She won't ever quit trying to steal my pups, the girl told herself. I'd better watch them close or she'll do it, too.

Two nights later, she did steal Skeezix. They had fed him in a pen, sealed with new chicken wire, so that he and Reddy would not fight over the food, and each would get his fill. Next morning, Skeezix was gone. The mother coyote had dug a hole beneath the wire and chewed his leash in two.

Although the discovery saddened Susy, she bore up well, chiefly because she still had Reddy. But she felt more uneasy than ever about him. Although Reddy was almost half-grown and his nose was becoming longer, his head flatter, and his yellow eyes more watchful and slitlike, he was still very dear to his real mother, Susy knew.

How big does Reddy have to get before that mother stops trying to get him back? the girl wondered.

In the days that followed, Susy lavished upon one coyote all the love and attention she had formerly devoted to two. And Reddy began to follow her everywhere, and to tolerate her touch, grinning widely when she reached down to run her right hand through the fur between his ears, and licking her fingers with his tongue.

He felt warm, and woolly, and intimate. Susy thought that she had never seen or touched a thing so delightful.

"*Ach*" she said softly, "having a coyote for a pet is *wunderlich*."

If she were inside the house and he was not, he would lie beneath the morning glory vine near the back step, listening for her voice, or watching for a quick glimpse of her head and shoulders as she passed a window while busy with household tasks.

Feeling his eyes upon her, the girl would pause at the window or open door and talk to him and the coyote would drop his head between his paws and look at her, his eyes shining, his bushy tail sweeping the ground, sending the dust and twigs flying.

One of their games was a special form of hide and seek. Admitting the coyote into the kitchen, Susy would go outside, shutting the door behind her. She would conceal herself in the shrubbery, or in the cyclone cellar or up in the barn loft. Then Rebecca would release the coyote.

Clapping his nose to the ground, Reddy would sniff up her trail at a trot, finding her with ridiculous ease.

Once Peter Zook sought to fool him by putting Susy before him on the buckskin and riding to the orchard so the girl could climb into a cherry tree off the horse's back, leaving no human trail upon the ground.

But when Peter rode back to the barn, dismounted, unsaddled the horse, turned him out, and walking back to the house, freed the coyote, Reddy raised his nose, caught Susy's scent in the tree fifty yards away and trotted straight to her.

"Yah!" laughed Peter, stamping his foot in the Amishman's gesture of amusement, "you smell too far, yet."

In spite of his regard for her the young coyote sometimes would stare thoughtfully into the distance. From deep in the prairie's stillness, a summons was sounding, a primordial pull that urged him to break his human ties, dash into the Wilderness and join his own kind. His attachment for the girl restrained him.

The yard became his playground. His eye caught the flight of every meadowlark or robin that flew across the lawn. His nose probed and tried to identify every smell.

Hating his leash, he found a way to deal with it. One morning, Susy took it off him and hung it on a nail in the shed. Reddy waited until she left, then leaped up and pulled it down. Using his sharp teeth, he severed it into three pieces, and buried each in a different spot of the yard.

But he had to be leashed when he could not be watched. Peter Zook made another, this one a wire that snapped onto a strong leather collar with brass brads. Now the coyote pup was securely tethered.

He retaliated by killing three of Rebecca's young

hens despite his shackles. They found only the white feathers near his box.

Disturbed, Rebecca clucked her tongue and began to watch him from her kitchen window but it was Susy who found out how he did it.

One morning when she took him a dish of table scraps, Reddy would not eat. Instead he lay down beside the dish, a queer look in his eyes. Susy was puzzled.

With her right hand, she tipped up his slender muzzle and looked into his eyes which were changing to greenish-yellow. His eyes always baffled her.

Usually they revealed some emotion—mischief, tenderness, independence, craft, and always a flash of wildness. But today they were masked, telling nothing.

"What's the matter with you?" Susy asked. "You don't look right. You sick?"

Deciding to scout him, she went into the house and watched out the bedroom window. She saw the coyote, still wearing the leash, take some of the food in his mouth and drop it near the chicken yard fence. Then he placed another fragment farther away and kept distributing it until he had laid a trail of food to his box. Then he reclined in the dust beside the box, pretending slumber.

With a whirring of wings, a young pullet flew over the fence. Cackling at her good fortune, she be-

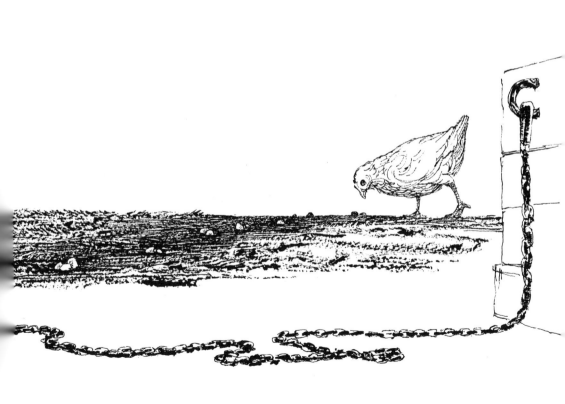

gan to eat the bits of food, walking to them one by one. The coyote crouched.

With a cry of alarm, Susy ran out the back door.

"Reddy!" she yelled, "No! No!" Her voice frightened away the pullet, saving its life.

"We've got to do something about that little scoundrel or we won't have any chickens yet," Rebecca fretted.

After that, the family called the coyote Susy's Scoundrel.

"My chickens and their eggs I can't give up," Rebecca added. "We need them to eat and sell. Why don't you let that wild thing go back to its maw?"

Dry mouthed from shock, Susy stared incredulously at her mother. Give up Reddy? Reddy was hers. He was part of the family. Those young hens had it coming. They flew around wild as guineas. Why didn't they stay in their own pens?

Her mother solved it temporarily by clipping the wing feathers of the pullets so they could not fly. But every time she saw the coyote, she shook her head and clucked her tongue.

Each day, Susy was permitted to bring Reddy into the house for short periods. On one of these occasions, Susy disobeyed her mother. Rebecca disciplined her by going straight to the seat of the problem with the back of a hair brush. Susy cried.

Then a diverting thing happened. Reddy ran to

the child and with a look of concerned sorrow on his face, sank back on his haunches, raised his nose, and began howling in short, yipping barks that finally cascaded together in the long lament that belongs so infallibly to the prairie buttes and hollows. The weird noise reverberated through the house.

Astonished, Rebecca stopped the punishment and Susy stopped her wailing that was far outdone by that of her sympathetic pet.

Afterward, the girl was elated. Reddy likes me, she thought happily. I don't think he will leave me now.

Reddy distrusted strangers. When Joe Schultz, the rural mail carrier, drove up in front and rattled the galvanized steel mail box while stuffing mail into it, Reddy ran behind the barn. But curiosity is a powerful emotion in a coyote. Cautiously, he slunk around through the garden. Hidden by a gooseberry bush, he watched the mail carrier depart.

"He's funny," laughed Susy, who had witnessed the incident. "When he runs away from something, he always comes back to a different place to look at what scared him."

But he didn't the next time he ran. He was running for his life.

It happened on the following Saturday morning. Peter Zook had ridden horseback into the river pasture to check on a newborn calf. Susy went along, riding behind her father on the saddle.

Reddy was permitted to accompany them. Swifter than any dog, he flashed everywhere at once, ranging on both sides of them to explore every thicket, moving faster and faster at the excitement of being free.

Suddenly, a patter of running feet approached. Instantly, Reddy's sharp ears were aware. Alert and alarmed, the half-grown coyote danced into the path ahead of the horse, looking back over his shoulder.

Then the hounds burst upon him. Reddy did not need prodding to be urged on his way. With a circular sweep of his tail, he flattened out his body and fled across the flats.

"They'll kill him!" screamed Susy, eyes wide with horror.

"Maybe not!" said Peter, reining down his horse, "Did you see him wind up his tail when he took off? He was flying."

He flanked the buckskin with his heels. "Hold tight, Susy! I don't think those dogs are in running shape. They can't be. It's too late in the season. Maybe we can see the race." They rode to the top of a knoll, where the view was plain.

The hounds ran in a long, loose-jointed line, their backs humping as they poured lightly up and down the coulees. Before them sped a tawny arrow— Reddy.

"Whoooo-eeeee!" yelled Peter Zook, slapping his leg with his hand. "Lookie at that thing fly!"

But Susy did not look. Instead, she turned her head and winked her eyes tightly shut. She remembered that her grandmother had once told her that she must not watch a friend pass from sight or she would never see him again.

Peter Zook stood anxiously in his stirrups, trying to see the race which was now out of sight behind a small hill. He reached around behind him, transferring Susy to his right hip and holding her firmly with one arm.

"Hang on, Susy!" he said. "That coyote in a minute will turn and take them back to the shed."

Steering the horse left-handed, he urged it forward. They galloped the half mile back to the farm. As they cantered into the driveway, Peter craned his neck, his eyes peering into the distance.

"Yep!" he shouted, "here they come!"

Dismounting, he put Susy on the ground. Side by side, they stood by the barn door, watching the race approach.

Treading familiar ground now, Reddy still led by thirty yards. But the foremost hounds were close. Susy stared, horrified. The coyote pup seemed far too small to be running it out with an adult hound pack.

"Red-deeeeee!" Susy shouted, her shrill voice pealing out strongly.

The coyote heard. Altering his course, he dodged beneath the lower bar of a plank fence. His toenails clicking across the concrete spillway behind the windmill, he headed straight for Susy. Fur ruffled, he leaped into the girl's arms, shivering and gasping for breath.

Carrying him, Susy ran into the barn and slammed the door shut, afraid the hounds might pluck him out of her grasp.

But the Zook dogs took care of that situation. With growls and gnashings of teeth, they pitched into the strange hounds. While half a dozen fights raged outside, Susy crouched inside, freeing Reddy. The coyote ran into his box and crouched in the back of it, white teeth bared.

"Leave him alone," warned Peter Zook, coming in to help, "Wait until he cools off."

A green pickup truck turned into the Zook driveway. In the road behind it lay a long cylinder of red dust.

A big man in a red sweater and jeans jumped out. Shouting and swearing, he soon separated his dogs from the Zook pack and flung them one by one into the back of his truck. Peter Zook helped him.

Susy came out of the shed staring at him, her finger in her mouth. The big man was Tige Ralston, a neighbor.

"Howdy, Zook," Tige Ralston called jovially. "Looks like my hounds invaded you."

"They got after our pet coyote," Peter Zook replied. "Maybe they picked up his trail as they followed us over to the river pasture. We went there to check on a calf."

"Pet coyote?" The cordiality went out of Tige Ralston's face. "Coyotes kill pigs and calves and sheep. Why are you sheltering this one?"

"My little girl wants this one for to play with," said Peter. He came forward, putting one hand on the fender of the green pickup. He looked like he did not enjoy what he next had to say.

"I would rather nobody hunted coyotes on my place," he said.

Tige Ralston frowned. "Why?"

"Because I want to protect them. They catch the rabbits and the other pests that eat my maize and my wheat. I wouldn't have much of a crop without them."

"And I wouldn't have much fun unless I chased 'em wherever my dogs jumped 'em," said Tige Ralston. "Last year, my dogs killed eight."

"A small bunch of hounds I keep," said Peter Zook. "It's good sport. My pack it's not near as good as yours. We've never caught a coyote yet. They're too smart for us."

Tige Ralston's eyes grew cold. "They're too smart for me, too," he said. "Last week, they found my sow and her litter and killed four baby pigs."

Peter Zook looked surprised. "I've never lost anything to a coyote," he said.

"Then you're blind as a mole. You can't see. You

know what they've been doing to Buck Karns' sheep."

Obviously offended, he climbed into his truck. "Better get up some signs if you aim to keep out hunters and dogs," he added. "But they might not do any good. A 'no trespassing' sign wouldn't stop the sheriff if he had to cross your property to catch a criminal. An' I doubt if they'd stop me iffen I got after a coyote I wanted real bad."

Remembering his religion which forbade violence or quarreling, Peter Zook stayed cool. His blue eyes brimmed with innocence and peace.

"That's good advice about the signs," he said, mildly. "I will some put up. And if I ever change my mind about other hunters and dogs on my land, I'll be glad to have you."

Tige Ralston did not reply. Twisting his starter key, he backed out of the driveway into the road, and drove off in an angry roar. Again the red dust climbed into a long cylinder behind him. Finger still in her mouth, Susy watched him out of sight.

Later when she put the leash on Reddy, he whined. Wagging his bushy tail, he licked her face. Peter Zook laughed.

"Look like we got us a young whippet here," he said. "Even if he is chust a baby, he can run like the dickens. Maybe we ought to enter him in the greyhound races at Wichita."

Susy knew that he was joking, but she did not share his levity. How could you enjoy watching a race in which half a dozen bloodthirsty hounds tried to kill something you loved? In the Wilderness, all the races with hounds were for life or death.

When she went out to feed Reddy the next morning, she discovered that they could not have entered him in the Wichita greyhound races even if they had wanted to.

Reddy was gone. The wire with the snap was still there, and so was the collar studded with brass brads. But it had been chewed in two. The coyote mother had won.

The little Amish girl sank to her knees in the straw of the shed and sobbed heartbrokenly.

Refusing to eat, Susy lay most of the morning in one of her mother's white beds in a back room, weeping and lamenting. Only when her father rocked her in his arms that night and sang to her an old German song did she finally cease her sobbing and go to sleep.

Peter Zook's voice wasn't musical but it exuded a tender comfort that Susy found most consoling. When her beloved doll Gracey was accidentally burned up in a trash fire, Susy's sorrow was overwhelming. Despite the fact that Gracey, like all Amish rag dolls, was faceless because the Amish rigidly enforce the scripture that says a "graven image violates God's will" Susy was so heartsick that she had to have her father's arms about her and she had to have that song.

It went like this:
"Charlotte, little Charlotte.
Come with me into the forest.
Where the birds are singing,
And the rabbits are dancing,
And the wind is blowing. . . ."

Many days passed before Suzy Zook stopped grieving over her lost pet and tried to take up the dull pattern of her life without him.

But every time she looked out her bedroom window upon the grayish-green sweep of the Wilderness, she thought of Reddy the coyote.

He was out there someplace. Would she ever see him again?

The Old One's Revenge

At first, Reddy stayed around the den, learning obedience and the tricks of survival that he should have mastered a month earlier.

His teacher was Smoky, his mother, whose fur was the same color as the yellowish smudge that arises from a prairie fire. Overjoyed to have recovered him, she spent much of her time that first day bringing him choice bits of food, washing him with her tongue, or just sitting a few feet off and looking at him with pride and happiness and silent love. And Reddy liked it.

Caution was an ingrained habit with her, he soon perceived, reflecting her high intelligence. She always approached the den against the wind, circling it warily and examining the ground for tracks. In the middle of the day, she would lie out of sight on a little hill, one hundred yards downwind from it, so that she could not only see and hear in all directions, but scent the air off her two pups, smelling any danger.

The den itself was designed to promote comfort and to thwart danger. Its outside approach was a gypsum ledge that extended out like a patio. When she came or departed, Smoky was careful to walk over it so that she would leave no telltale tracks.

Reddy liked his subterranean home. Dark and cool, it consisted of a tunnel, dug by the mother, that reached far underground. An air hole concealed in a clump of yucca admitted fresh air directly over the nest. She had located its entrance on a southeast slope so that the pups could come out and enjoy the sunshine.

Smoky also had another den half a mile away that she used for purposes of strategy. When she knew that she was sighted from a distance by hunters, she would let them see her enter it while carrying food to her pups. Then she would leave by an alternate exit hidden from the view of her pursuers and proceed by a meandering course to her hungry children.

Reddy and Skeezix spent hours each day playing outside the den. They romped with Smoky, chasing her and biting at her fur. They wrestled each other in mock battle, rolling and tumbling in the grass. They snapped at each other's feet and tails. Giddy with pleasure, they whirled round and round clockwise, then spun in the opposite direction, thrusting up their heads and barking joyfully.

The first time the big buff-gray dog coyote trotted up, a rabbit in his jaws, and dropped it in the sand, Reddy snarled, bared his fangs and retreated to the mouth of the den.

But when he saw his brother Skeezix go fearlessly to the stranger and pick up the rabbit without any retaliatory action from him, Reddy realized that the newcomer presented no problem and belonged to the group.

Ignoring Reddy's unfriendliness, Buff, the big stranger, moved with regal majesty and carried his head high. Unlike the fathers of many other animals, the coyote sire is devoted to his young, and helps the mother feed and protect them.

Suddenly, Buff's ears flicked forward and he stood, front feet spread, nose lifting and palpitating. A low growl escaped him. The mother and both cubs scurried into the den, which had another opening concealed by brush. The father followed. A minute passed.

Jud Bodkins, the wolfer, rode up on his black

horse. Perspiration glistened on his hairy face.

"Wah!" he commanded, pulling his horse to a halt. Frowning, he scrutinized the area for tracks.

Smoky, the coyote mother, had already tricked him twice that day, planting fresh tracks around half a dozen dens in the area. Laboring in the July heat, Jud had dug out two of them but found nothing.

He suspected that he would find nothing here, too, but his thirst for liquor was so intolerable that he put his hand on the shovel tied to his saddle. Then growling a curse, he gave up the idea and rode on. He was tired of digging empty holes.

Before the first graying of dawn, Smoky conducted Reddy and Skeezix on a tour of the spring-greened Wilderness terrain. She first taught them to return to the den without using their eyes. This was achieved by backtracking their own trail, nose to the ground, because a coyote can trail as delicately as a hound.

She showed them how to choose their path once they had decided which way they would go for the daily killing. Steering by the peaks of the small red hills, they avoided barren areas where a rifle might cut them down, and used weeds, sage, yucca, ditches, and sparse timber for concealment. She showed them how to camouflage themselves against the scantiest vegetation and never to kill near the den, for fear of drawing to themselves a retaliatory strike by men.

She taught them to move with extreme caution around farms and ranches. A good way to kill around human habitations, Reddy learned, was to hunt in pairs and use teamwork. Crouching in the sage with Skeezix, Reddy watched Buff show himself, drawing all the dogs after him, while Smoky glided in from the opposite direction and picked off a chicken, a duck, or a goose.

Smoky trained them to assure safety by stopping often to look both ahead and behind for movement by an enemy. Reddy's eyes, ears, and nose functioned so intelligently that soon he learned to analyze what he saw, heard, or smelled, whether it was the whisper of a field mouse running or the scent of a meadowlark's droppings that told him that the bird had gone by recently and might be just ahead.

The art of small game hunting was another lesson emphasized by Smoky, for the chief object of a coyote's life is the satisfying of a hunger that is always pinching, and to this aim all the animal's cunning is directed.

She showed them how to spring into the air to trap grasshoppers and how to point a covey of quail like a setter, then pounce into the center of it, and try to seize a bird.

She halted at a creek, and using a forepaw, scooped live minnows out of the shallows for them to eat. When she crossed the creek by wading through the shallows, Reddy followed her dutifully. Skeezix, who liked water, plunged into the deepest part and swam across, then emerged without shaking himself.

All summer long, Smoky's instruction continued for soon the pups would do their own hunting. With only two offspring to school, the mother could devote more time to each, and her training included refinements that would not have been possible with a brood of six or seven.

She taught them how to drive cottontails into a closely strung barbed wire fence, stunning them. Reddy learned that automobiles on a highway provide food, and how to search the highway at night or early morning for the carcasses of fresh-killed possums and skunks blinded by the headlights.

He found that he liked the tart taste of the wild sand plums Smoky taught him to find in the grass beneath the bushes. He learned that cattle are the friends of coyotes, and that by walking behind a cow grazing in tall grass or weeds, he could pounce on the mice she flushed.

And while traveling about the Wilderness absorbing all this, Reddy was becoming familiar with every hillock and trench and path through the sage. He was learning the game trails, the cattle trails, the old roads, and the gullies that comprise the avenues of escape. He learned where to hunt, where to find water, where to hide. He was fixing a map of it all in the back of his head, until soon he knew the area as well as a house dog knows its own backyard.

But hunting was not all he lived for. Coyotes take pleasure in their games by starlight and afterward proclaim their mad joy by yelping sociably to the moon which, like a huge orange, thrusts itself above the prairie's eastern rim.

In the cool of the evenings, Reddy and Skeezix ran races across the prairie with another family of young coyotes. No matter what the length of these dashes, Reddy always won.

Racing became his favorite pastime. Anything might start it—a low-flying bird, a leaf blown by the breeze, or a cloud drifting across the prairie.

Recalling his run with Tige Ralston's hounds, he longed to try himself once more against them. He was older and fleeter now. He could do better than just hold his own. Soon he was covering ground at a devastating pace. Ears laid back and bushy tail streaming, he flowed over the flats like an arrow twanged from an Indian's bow, skimming the prairie with no lost bounding motion.

One day, they saw men with greyhounds. Smoky gave a low cry of warning and dropped in her tracks. Greyhounds hunt by sight, rather than smell, and can discern a moving object half a mile away.

Eager to race, Reddy whined imploringly and

looked at her for permission. Smoky fanged him sharply. Chastened, he hunkered down obediently, the sting of her teeth smarting in his shoulder. But he still longed to test his speed against the hounds.

Later, Buff joined them, emerging noiselessly from the sage. He and Smoky led the two pups to a nearby expanse of sun-burned shortgrass where a new phase of their instruction began—stalking prairie dogs. Reddy had never seen such curious animals.

Three acres of land bordering the Wilderness had been undermined by these odd little creatures who sat upon the earthen mounds above their burrows, and folding their front paws meekly in front of them, defied the coyotes with thin, sharp cries, much like the squeak of a toy rabbit when it is pinched.

With Reddy and Skeezix observing from a nearby hill, Smoky hid in a gully at the outskirts of the prairie dog town. The trap was set.

Buff trotted boldly into the center of the village. With an alarmed chattering, all the nearby prairie dogs dove into their holes. While they were out of sight, Smoky ran forward, like a pale yellowish ghost, staying upwind and hiding behind a clump of greasewood near the burrow that was to be her target. From the top of the hill, Reddy studied the maneuver with the utmost interest.

Buff strolled leisurely through the settlement. As

he did so, the prairie dogs he had passed began to emerge cautiously, only their eyes showing above their burrows.

The fat one whose burrow was nearest Smoky's hiding place raised his head an inch, then another, until he seemed satisfied that Buff, the only enemy in sight, no longer constituted a threat.

He hopped upon his observation mound, took another look and barked with satisfaction. Buff was moving farther and farther away. He decided to resume feeding. Since the grass around his burrow was scant, he had to go fifteen feet from the door of his home to find the thicker turf.

Twice he started, and twice jerked himself back, his fat little body twitching timidly. Finally he conquered his fear. After another searching look, he scampered to the feeding place. Vibrating with energy, he plunged his face into the herbage.

Watching him from forty feet away, Smoky crept slowly forward, moving so smoothly and deliberately that she seemed drawn on silent wheels. Every time he raised his face from the grass, she froze into stone. Soon she had cut the forty feet to twenty and still he had not seen her.

On the hill, Reddy gathered himself into a convulsive knot. Now was the time!

Behind the greasewood bush, Smoky exquisitely

timed the climax. Dashing from her hiding place, she bagged Mr. Prairie Dog in half a dozen strides. And Reddy never forgot.

That first summer, Reddy seemed to spend all his time learning, evaluating, and memorizing. His instruction continued into the fall.

A coyote gets his guile from four principal sources. He is born with the cunning of his clan. He is trained by his parents, particularly by his mother. He learns from his comrades and associates. And he benefits from his own personal experience.

In September, when the air was full of wasps and the sumac was turning scarlet, Reddy learned that good company, as well as good sport, is an essential part of coyote sociability. So he hunted not only with Skeezix and their parents, but occasionally with a young Texas coyote who was a year older than he.

Richly colored, this coyote was the smallest and handsomest of all the varieties that frequented the Wilderness country. His legs and feet were orangish all the way around. He had small teeth and a small skull. At the slightest alarm his ears would stand as erect as a terrier's. His hide showed the scars of healed rattlesnake bites.

In the races the young coyotes ran, this fellow gave Reddy his closest competition, although Reddy always won.

When food became scarce in late summer, it was

the Texas coyote accustomed to life on the desert who showed Reddy a new source of supply. It happened while they were resting early one afternoon near a pasture owned by Buck Karns, who operated the biggest sheep ranch in the area, an expanse of eleven sections.

A noise as of dead leaves rustling came to Reddy. He raised his head and looked. The Texas coyote had heard it, too, and was on his feet sniffing and pawing the leaves near the sound.

Suddenly, he jumped back. His ears twitched and his tail wagged. Cautiously, he approached from a different angle.

With his teeth, he began to tear apart the long grass. Finding an opening, he thrust his head into it, sniffing and wagging his tail. Again he pawed the grass and again he sprang back.

Interested now, Reddy joined him and saw a bull snake coiled about the base of a small scrub oak.

The Texas coyote sprang forward, seized the snake by its tail, dragged it into the open, and released it. The snake coiled itself and raised its head a foot above the grass, ready for battle.

The snake struck at the coyote. The coyote dodged back, then flashed forward, snapping the snake just back of the head, and jumping out of range. Reddy whined, wishing that he could have some of the action, too. It looked like fun.

Twice the snake flung its head like the lash of a slingshot, but so fast were the coyote's movements that it was not hit. Each time the snake struck, the coyote dodged, then leaped forward and snapped the snake's neck. Finally, the coyote shook the snake until it stopped squirming.

Satisfied that his victim was dead, the Texas coyote sat down, scanning the terrain warily in all directions. Then he began to eat the snake, starting with its head. Reddy watched, enthralled.

Another of Reddy's associates was one the Wilderness hunters called Old Social Security. For years they had chased him vainly. He was too smart to let them get close to him with a hound pack. The dogs always had to start from too far away.

Despite his age, the Old One had amazing stamina. He could run all night. And he always took the hounds to the section line roads where they had difficulty smelling his trail, even when the owners would put their dog's nose in his track.

"He's got too much milk in his coconut," said Wolf Thompson, a wiry little farmer who followed his hounds barefoot. But they all kept trying. Great honor would fall upon the hunter who finally took the Old One's ears.

It was the Old One who introduced Reddy to Charley Huff's yellow-meated watermelon patch. All summer, Reddy had seen the green-striped melons growing in the Huff field behind the barn. But he did not know their delicious secret.

On a night radiant with moonlight, the Old One escorted Reddy to the Huff melon patch, located just three hundred yards south of the Cannonball, the hard-surfaced automobile highway leading to the town of White Bead.

When he saw the man standing guard in the middle of the melons, Reddy hung back—even if the man did not have a gun. And when the Old One trotted so close to the man that he carelessly brushed against him, Reddy crouched in terror and dug his toenails into the sand, prepared to flee.

Then he noticed that no human smell came off the figure and that it was only a wooden contrivance dressed in ragged clothing. He followed the Old One into the field. It was laced with the striped fruit which, except for its larger size, greatly resembled the gourd.

But it did not taste like a gourd, Reddy discovered. When he sampled the cool sweetness of his first yellow heart, he felt a blissful melting within him. It was a treat to tantalize the tongue.

The Old One had a way of unerringly selecting the mellow ones. After clawing the outer skin and smelling the pulp within, he knew whether the melons were ripe or green. Reddy sniffed the clawed places, too. He wanted to remember that identifying smell.

A dog's outraged barking violated the quiet. A

brown staghound, big as a small calf, burst upon them.

As they ran through the orchard, pursued by this noisy sentinel, a shotgun roared, belching a rope of fire ahead of them.

Reddy had never heard a shotgun before, especially one at such close quarters. With a convulsive leap, he sprang into the air as if safety lay in the fleecy clouds drifting across the moon's face. But he lit running.

Later, the Old One barked and Reddy found him in a nearby cornfield. They looked sheepishly at each other. Although their muzzles were still daubed with the yellow meat of the melon, each had only begun to eat. And the hunger pangs pinched harder than ever.

The Old One sat down and chewed a sandburr out of one foot. For the past seven summers he had supped on those melons as if they were his own. He had not used them wastefully but had dined only upon what was needed to satisfy a reasonable appetite. Clearly, the incident grated upon him.

Reddy dug at a flea in his shoulder fur. His ears still rang from the gun's thunderclap.

Four nights later, the Old One again led Reddy on a raid of Charley Huff's goodies.

This time, the coyotes investigated with meticulous care, twice circling the house, barn, orchard, and the melon patch as they probed the air for the scent of a man hiding with a gun. All they found was a human footprint, very stale.

Then the Old One did something that surprised Reddy. Instead of heading silently for the melon patch and its feast of yellow hearts, the Old One raised his head toward the house and barked once softly. Instantly, the big brown staghound awoke and invited himself to the party, charging noisily upon them.

This time, the oldster took pains to lead the chase away from the orchard. Through a field of alfalfa, he ran east, Reddy at his shoulder. As they glided along, the Old One threw one shrewd look back at the pursuing hound, as if he wanted to be sure they were being followed. And Reddy wondered what devilry his companion might be hatching.

Soon the coyotes reached the Cannonball highway. Instead of crossing it, the Old One turned right and ran along the bar ditch paralleling the asphalt road. The staghound drew within twenty-five yards, running wild.

A pair of automobile headlights shone in the distance, coming toward them. The Old One shot a look over his left shoulder. All clear there. No cars were coming from that direction. But the staghound surely was!

With the approaching auto only thirty yards away, the Old One broke suddenly across the highway in front of it. Reddy followed. Both coyotes had the distance carefully gauged and were not hit.

Thump!

Brakes squeaked. The car lurched and rolled to a stop. A door slammed and a man got out, swearing.

"How dumb can a danged dog get?" Although Reddy did not know what the man was saying, he knew that hounds had no sense about their running. Peter Zook's hounds, or Tige Ralston's, or anybody's else. You could never tell when one would gallop himself to death in the heat, or collide with a tree.

Back to the melon patch trotted the two coyotes. Again they made their cautious circle, testing all the sights and sounds and smells. No cause for alarm.

As he bit into his second yellow heart, his nose pushing gently against its sweetness, Reddy stole a look at the arch-conspirator feasting by his side.

In the moonlight, the Old One's face, lathered with juicy watermelon, gleamed with satisfaction.

The Fight by the Culvert

From the lip of the arroyo that hid him, Reddy saw ranger J. C. Clack's brown stetson hat bobbing up and down above the horizon as he walked about the barn lot doing his chores.

Even though the ranger was downwind and dressed in clothing that blended with the Wilderness coloration, Reddy spotted him a quarter of a mile away by his foolish hopping up and down like a kangaroo rat.

Clack's farm, a modest spread that fronted the Wilderness, boasted a six-room brick home, behind which lay the showpiece of Poncho County, a concrete swimming pool.

The state ranger could not have afforded this luxury on his salary, but Mrs. Clack had inherited considerable wealth, and the pool had been built with some of this money. Clack also owned a kennel of greyhounds and a stable of quarter horses. Mrs. Clack raised purebred Plymouth Rock hens.

Reddy and his brother Skeezix knew all about the Clack home and about the hounds, chickens, and horses. And also about Sam, the fierce-looking young German police dog who ruled the yard. And they knew about the Clacks themselves, and their three children, too.

As far as that was concerned, Reddy was beginning to know the people in every house that adjoined the Wilderness: whether the owner could shoot straight, whether his wife would shoot at all, how far their bullets would reach, where the hounds were kept, and whether the yard dogs were formidable or only annoying. Reddy watched and studied everything and everybody.

Now he was even studying Skeezix who lay beside him in the arroyo. Reddy saw that his ash-colored brother had his eye on that swimming pool filled to the curbs with cool blue water. It was late September, the mercury stood at ninety-four, and Skeezix liked to swim.

Ranger Clack had ridden off in his black pickup truck. Reddy knew that he would be gone most of the morning checking the windmills in his pastures. The hounds were securely penned. Mrs. Clack, who was afraid of guns, was busy inside the house.

That left only Sam, the young German police dog, and Skeezix had plans for Sam.

Staying downwind from the kennels of the hounds, the two coyotes trotted cautiously to a point where the sage stopped and the Clack's buffalo grass lawn started.

There Reddy lay prone, concealed by the sage, and watched everything carefully. His mother's prudence strong within him, he wanted no part of what Skeezix was about to undertake.

Skeezix trotted boldly toward Sam, who at once raised a storm of barking and rushed at him. Skeezix gave a few rods of ground, then charged Sam furiously, whereupon Sam retreated, then turned at bay, growling and showing all his teeth.

Then Skeezix did a daring thing. He deliberately laid down on his stomach, facing the dog. He was panting leisurely. It's too hot to fight, he seemed to say. Let's be friends.

Sam wanted none of that. He was protector of the Clack house and grounds, and it was being invaded.

He charged again, whereupon the coyote rolled over on his back, thrust up all four paws, wagged his tail and whined entreatingly. Fur ruffled with fear, Reddy watched from the sage.

At first, Sam did not know what to make of the young coyote's advances. But he halted his belligerence. From the arroyo, Reddy could see the dog change his mind.

Sam's tail began to twitch and move repeatedly back and forth. Then he began to bounce stiffly off his front feet and to sway his shoulders, becoming the soul of good fellowship. Soon he and the coyote were playing together around the front lawn. Skeezix kept angling toward the swimming pool.

In another five minutes, he was in it, joyously drinking and splashing and swimming while Sam stood with his head cocked and his front feet on the curb, puzzled by the odd behavior of his guest. Sam was never permitted in the family pool.

Frightened and bemused by turns, Reddy continued to stare from his cover. He saw the ranger's wife emerge suddenly from the back door, waving a broom at Skeezix.

"Scat, you bold thing!" she yelled. Skeezix was already out of the pool and fleeing with his ears laid back.

He scatted, all right. But on the way he picked up one of her gray Plymouth Rock hens with bluish-black striped feathers before gliding toward Reddy and the open sage.

"Oh!" she shouted in horror. "It got one of my chickens! It's a coyote! Sic him, Sam!" Sam ran forward a few steps, then stopped and looked at her in confusion, swinging his tail from side to side.

As the two coyotes fled, Reddy looked askance at his brother. After a depredation like that, they would not dare approach Clack's again for several weeks.

That his coyote parents loved him and would die for him Reddy soon found out. Coyote fathers and mothers are family people. Because of their intelligence and their affection for their young, larger numbers of their litters grow to maturity than do those of other predatory animals.

It is in the summer that many of the half-grown pups are killed. Just beginning to run alone, they are easily trapped or shot. In his hunting forays, Reddy saw an occasional coyote corpse wired mockingly to a fence, white teeth gleaming eerily in the sunshine, attesting to the peril all coyotes faced from the aroused farmers and ranchers.

Before sunup on a cloudy morning in October, Reddy, Skeezix, and Smoky were hunting in an alfalfa field along the west flank of the Wilderness. Suddenly, as they came over a hill, they saw hounds and two mounted riders before them. Too late, Smoky gave a low cry of warning and froze, dropping to her stomach.

A greyhound had seen them and the whole pack charged toward them, swallowing the ground in long strides.

Whining to her pups to follow her, Smoky turned back toward the Wilderness canyons. Skeezix ran with her. Reddy shot joyously for the open prairie, accepting the challenge of the chase.

His mother barked a sharp warning, but he paid no attention. A brown and white spotted hound began to gain on Reddy. Like a graceful puff of smoke, Reddy's mother put on a burst of speed, came up behind the hound, and grabbing him by the ham of his right leg, threw him in a cloud of dust. Jumping up, the dog blindly continued the chase.

Abandoning her safer course, Smoky cut across to intercept Reddy. For half a mile, her speed was breathtaking. She was pouring out the last of it to save him.

Ever since she had recovered the red pup, she had tried to teach him caution, and to temper the carelessness he had acquired through contact with human beings. But Reddy's weakness was his pride in his getalong. He thought he could outrun anything on four legs.

When his mother spurted up to his shoulder, nipped him with her teeth, and tried to bump him toward the cover of the canyons, Reddy ran out his tongue and laughed at her. It was invigorating to feel the buffalo grass flying beneath his pads and the smell of the sun-heated sage in his nostrils.

The hounds gained steadily. Smoky, fearing for the red pup's life, deliberately slowed until the dogs drew within forty yards. Then she cut straight behind Reddy, swinging to the left. All the dogs followed her.

Reddy, looking back over his shoulder, realized in a flash the purpose of her strategy and saw that he had lost his competitors and his fun. Veering back toward Smoky and the chase, he lengthened out, gained on her, came in from the side between her and the hounds, and with a great dash of speed, crossed behind her.

Triumph surged through him. Now the hounds again were following him. They always followed the coyote that cut across behind the one in front. This was an interesting discovery and Reddy never forgot it. He had also discovered that he could outrun his mother.

Now was the time to outrun the dogs, too. He had enjoyed the racing but prolonging it might be foolhardy. He did not want his body decorating some rancher's fence, food for the crows and the buzzards.

Rotating his tail in a quick explosive circle that seemed to give him the centrifugal force of a whirlwind, he reached down inside himself and called upon all his rapidity of movement. The hound pack began to drop back.

As Reddy ran, he saw opportunity after opportunity to slip them with his guile: a cutbank that opened into a creek with cool wet sand, a gully that led to a gypsum hole where they would never find him, a herd of friendly cattle that he could run through and they could not. He abandoned all this for the greater joy of defeating them with pure running, the fastest they had ever seen.

Reddy loved to run. In half an hour of straight running, he could get a nose full of smells that he could not otherwise scent in a whole day. He liked seeing the yucca and the turpentine weed fly by. He liked looking back over his shoulder and seeing the frustration in the faces of the pursuers.

Behind him, his mother slowed to a trot, watching with fear and dismay. She knew exactly what he was thinking.

All young coyotes, soon as they find out how fast their legs will carry them, believe with reckless optimism that no creature in the world can run them down. But greyhounds are not ordinary creatures.

Swiftness and stamina are born in them, whetted by frequent hunts under a master's guidance. Once they overhaul a victim, they become implacable killers. Smoky feared that the red pup would be overtaken and killed.

But when she and Skeezix reached the home den, Reddy lay relaxed and contented in the sand, letting the south wind ruffle his wet fur.

When he saw his mother, he whined and dropped his head contritely between his forepaws, remembering that he had incurred her displeasure. Facing him, she growled in the back of her throat, scolding him in the language of the pack. She nipped his shoulder.

Reddy tried to make himself even flatter, his eyes staring pleadingly into hers. Only when she lowered her head and with her moist tongue began to groom his ears and forehead did he feel that he was forgiven. Slowly, his bushy tail began to sweep back and forth, scattering the sand.

At five months, a coyote is old enough to take care of himself. Reddy had begun to look like an adult.

His nose was long and pointed and his eyes set in dark spectacle frames. His copperish fur was picking up glints of rust and black. His teeth had become ivory needles that could cut as cleanly as a guillotine. His gape had such astonishing width that his mouth looked as if it were opened to the back of his neck.

As he grows older, a coyote's aim in life is not only to fill its stomach, but to rear a family, love it, and teach it to survive against the trapper, the hunter, and the hound pack.

It was now October, time for those invading hound packs. The tempo of Reddy's training was stepped up and with it an increase in the number of his brushes with death. Smoky taught him to act smartly and coolly in all such crises until soon these encounters became almost routine. But the peril was always there. A single miscalculation meant a coyote life expunged.

Once when a hound pack pursued them closely, Smoky guided Reddy and Skeezix at a dead run through a growth of shinnery, then cut suddenly to the left, skirting it, and returning to the place where they had entered. To Reddy's surprise, the hounds poured on over the hill in the original direction.

Smoky did not linger. Quickly, she led them into a gully, out of sight, and kept them moving. She knew that a sensible greyhound losing sight of its quarry will circle, or run to a hill or knoll so that it can again spot the coyote and resume the chase.

Coyotes usually hunt at night and early in the morning, and spend much of the day resting out of sight. Most of the hound packs came on Saturday; it was then that a coyote needed all the sagacity he could muster.

Reddy soon learned when it was Saturday by watching Tige Ralston's farm early in the mornings. School had started in the adjacent town of White Bead. If Tige drove out of his yard in the yellow school bus that picked up children all along the road, Reddy knew that the hunters would be few. But if Tige departed in his green pickup truck, with his dog box in the back, it was Saturday. That spelled trouble for the coyote world.

To a man, the Wilderness looked bleak and desolate and inhospitable. But to a coyote there was enchantment in the roominess, the silences, and the boundless skies. There was food, a home, and companions.

At daybreak, standing wet legged in the shadows, Reddy could see the fresh deer droppings and smell the musk odor of the doe and fawn that had gone by earlier. Later, he liked to run leisurely through the buffalo grass so laden with dew that it glistened whitely in the morning sunshine, feeling its wetness between his toes, and reading the Wilderness sights and sounds and smells as a man would read a newspaper.

On the sweltry afternoons, there would be a bird gasping with his bill open in the shadow of every fence post. And in the shank of the afternoon, when the hawks would begin to swoop low over the sage, Reddy knew that the mice were moving along their secret paths and that it was time for him to start his hunting, too.

This land could have given him and his family the seclusion they craved. But because of the continuous lamb slaying, and the determination of the ranchers to block it by destroying the entire coyote population, that was not to be.

One afternoon a storm threatened, but after spattering the prairie with a few large drops, it blew around the shoulder of the ridge. The sunlight returned and when its golden beams darted down from behind a black cloud, like spokes from the bottom half of a wheel, the Wilderness seemed smoking with mist.

Buff, Reddy, and Skeezix were hunting near the river when Lige Lancaster's hounds suddenly appeared from behind a butte. The three coyotes gave ground before them, only to run into another pack coming from the east.

Surprised at so many dogs so close, Reddy bounded lightly into the air, looking for an exit. Tucking his tail between his legs, he turned to his father for guidance. In what direction did Buff wish to run?

To Reddy's astonishment, Buff chose not to run at all. Without taking his eyes off the dogs, he snarled a warning to Reddy over his shoulder. Then he backed up against a fence surrounded by Russian thistles and faced his enemies fearlessly.

Deciding to support his father, Reddy ran into a metal culvert nearby, where they could encounter their foes one at a time. He peeped out anxiously, wondering why Buff had not joined him. With one of them defending it from each end, the culvert seemed much safer. Skeezix had chosen to run and apparently had got clean away.

But Buff was staying in the open. The chines on his back rose, his shoulder blades stiffened, and his ears flattened ominously.

Come on, he seemed to taunt the dogs. I'm going

to fight you while I'm fresh, not when I'm exhausted at the end of a chase. And this is as good a place as any.

That suited the dogs. One and two at a time, they flung themselves upon him, going for his throat, flanks, feet—anything they could get hold of. From the opening of the culvert, Reddy watched with awe. All the dogs outweighed Buff.

Knocked off balance by the original onslaught, Buff's tail whipped in a circle as he turned himself in midair, barely avoiding a thrust at his jugular. Then the big dog coyote began to fight. His scissorlike jaws snapped vigorously. The light in his eyes was that of battle, not of fear.

He gashed a greyhound's shoulder but took a nick on his own in return. He cut deeply into another dog's foot and with a howl of pain the dog limped from the fight.

A black hound grabbed him behind the neck. With an incredibly savage shake, Buff hurled him off and locked jaws with another antagonist, hanging on until his throat became endangered again, retreating a step, and slashing viciously to right and left.

A tan hound kept trying to enter the culvert while lying on his side, but Reddy had no trouble defending it since the drain measured only eighteen inches in diameter. He was doing so well that he had time to see much of the battle outside.

Outside, Buff had won back that lost step with a furious counterattack during which his teeth clashed like knives. Whining with frustration, the pack rushed again and again. This was close-up warfare that the buff-gray coyote understood very well. He crouched low to the ground, his body humped into a ball, and concentrated on not letting them put him on his back.

Suddenly, Buff sprang sideways and running to the culvert's mouth, he faced his attackers from new ground. The hounds rushed from all sides, but Reddy came out and fought fiercely at his father's flank. Then both coyotes retreated into the culvert, Buff taking one end and Reddy the other. The hounds began to lose interest.

Finally Lige Lancaster called off his dogs. "They're cut up pretty bad, and I didn't bring no gun," he apologized.

"I didn't neither," said the other farmer. "We'll never get them coyotes out of that tin horn."

At the den that night, with the rest of the family watching, Buff strutted about with his tail suspended high in the air. He licked his wounds and arched his back with pride. Although he limped badly, he did so with a swaggering sense of triumph, striding on his toes.

The easiest coyote to trap is a young male. Smoky took Reddy and Skeezix on a tour of Jud Bodkin's trap lines so they might see the danger firsthand.

Despite his general worthlessness, Jud Bodkins was smart with traps. Now that all coyote pups had grown too big to inhabit the dens, the wolfer had tripled the number of small traps he had sown about the Wilderness. More and more coyote scalps without ears decorated the fence lines.

For bait, Jud was now using decayed horse meat which he set out while wearing cotton gloves. He boiled in sage tea those traps he set in the sage to neutralize the human scent.

Smoky was the prize he most wanted because she had eluded him so many times. Through his binoculars, he had seen her using a certain passageway beneath a fence when she exited from a pasture. He knew that she used it regularly.

His most cunningly laid trap was a blind one he buried shallowly at this exit spot. But Smoky saw the bruised grass, and walking around the contrivance with her pups, she changed her route a few feet south. Next day, he set a trap there, but she walked around it, too.

Finally, he set a maze of six traps about the area, burying in their midst a prairie dog he had shot, and concealing everything.

To this perilous lure, Smoky conducted Reddy and Skeezix, showing them each trap in turn and growling a warning to them that they must not touch any of them.

Then stepping within inches of two of the traps,

she dug up the prairie dog. Fearing poison, she growled her sons away from it and left it on the prairie as a warning to the wolfer that he'd best stop trying to belittle her intelligence.

They resumed their tour of Jud Bodkins' trap line. Of the traps sprung, one held the shriveled carcass of a crow and another the chewed-off paw of a coyote. Ears laid back thoughtfully, Reddy studied that chewed-off forepaw.

A distressed barking sounded ahead. Investigating, they came upon a pathetic sight.

A dog coyote, as big as Buff, stood facing them, his front foot caught in a trap. Starved and emaciated, he apparently had been there for days, while Jud Bodkins stayed home consuming the whisky his coyote scalps had purchased.

Almost insane with rage and fear, he was snapping at the flies that bothered him. He would jump high into the air, or make a run on the trap chain and be jerked back into a somersault. Desperate, he had even begun to gnaw off his trapped foot.

Whining with compassion, Reddy stood watching until Smoky finally pointed them home.

All through the night, Reddy heard the captured coyote barking for its mate. Next morning, he and Skeezix, hunting in the area, saw Jud Bodkins riding his black horse toward the noise. Soon, the trapped animal began barking wildly and Reddy knew that it had sighted the wolfer and probably realized its fate.

The crack of a rifle silenced everything. Later, the big coyote's body, minus the ears, swung from the top wire of a fence. And Reddy never forgot.

He was becoming aware that war had been declared on all his kind by the farmers and ranchers of Poncho County. The next day he would encounter the cause of the war, the coyote killer whose murders had brought all the grief down upon his clan.

In Buck Karns' Pasture

The day had started as had so many in Reddy's young life, with Smoky still schooling him and Skeezix in the techniques of survival. It was late October now, and the hunters were everywhere.

She had got them out early. With her tongue, she was licking the fur into place behind their ears, as a human mother wets down a cowlick in a child's unruly hair. Although annoyed by her ministrations—he was now six months old—Reddy submitted to them. He still was subject to her authority.

The eastern sky was streaked in lavender and yellow when they first heard the baying of the hound.

It was a deep, resonant baying and Reddy knew from the way the dog took scent and cried in the same breath that it was running. He had never heard a hound making music on a hot trail and did not know the danger it portended. But Smoky knew.

She knew that a baying hound is one who can sniff your track right up to the door of your den, and bring a whole pack of greyhounds with him.

With a low cry, she dropped to the ground and began to lick the bottoms of all four of her feet. Whining at Reddy and Skeezix, she signaled them to do the same. The pack was still three hundred yards away.

Reddy didn't understand this new maneuver, but still he sat on his buttocks and tongued his feet as Smoky wished. He did not want to be bitten or growled at.

The delay cost them seventy-five yards, but it was time well spent. Smoky took them to the nearby county road, a hard dirt highway with a minimum of traffic. After racing one hundred yards down it, she left it with a long leap into a sandy field. Reddy and Skeezix followed.

Reddy sensed that her strategy was somehow connected with concealing their scent, but he did not see why that was necessary.

A hound had to see you before it could chase you, he thought. Then he remembered that his mother had a good reason for everything she did. So he did as she asked, storing the incident and all its unanswered details within his fertile mind. Behind them, the baying ceased.

In mid-afternoon, Reddy and Skeezix were resting beneath a sage clump when again they heard the baying of a hound. High and piercing, this voice was different from that they had heard in the morning. Again Reddy could tell that the dog was running and probably chasing something.

Reddy was not worried. The voice had nothing to do with them. Even if the pack ranged close, all they had to do was lie still and they wouldn't be seen.

The baying became louder. Reddy cocked his big ears toward it, listening curiously. Skeezix whined and looked inquiringly at Reddy.

Let's get out of here, Skeezix seemed to say. Reddy crouched, dropping his head between his forepaws. Why were the hounds coming this way? The hounds couldn't see them. With all the Wilderness to hunt in, the hounds would surely swing off in another direction.

Suddenly a black hound, nose down, voice in full

cry, broke around a cedar and headed straight for Reddy. Reddy snuggled lower, blending his body against the red earth. He knew that he had not been seen because the hound was looking at the ground.

"Booooo! Booooo! Booooo!" it yodeled and leaped upon him.

Reddy hurled himself to one side and tried to run but with momentum up, the dog caught him easily. Reddy felt its teeth seize his upper right leg and he was conscious of a weight fastened to him.

Off balance, he fell and saw a greyhound menacing Skeezix. Wheeling, he slashed the black hound across the nose and its weight dropped off him.

Free, he tried to brush around a greasewood bush but now there were greyhounds everywhere.

"Boooooooo!" bawled the black hound almost in his ear. Again, he felt its teeth in his right rear leg. Again he was thrown and released.

Rolling to his feet, he bared his fangs but the black hound just walked off and quit the fight. I've done my job, it seemed to say to the greyhounds. The rest is up to you.

Two greyhounds charged Reddy. He jumped between them and shot for the open prairie. Twenty yards to his left, Skeezix was fleeing from three greyhounds, his ash-colored tail floating out behind him. Skeezix's plight was desperate. Although he was cutting and dodging, he was about to be caught.

They're going to run him down, Reddy realized. If they do, they will kill him. I've got to help him.

Summoning all his speed, Reddy veered to his left, running so low that his stomach brushed the grass. He overhauled the greyhound nearest Skeezix, a big fellow wearing a brown collar. This was his first chance to study a greyhound from close proximity. He could see the muscles rippling in its brisket, back, and legs. Its flanks were lean as a snake's. Its long ears were strung out behind its head like the loose ends of Peter Zook's wool muffler when he galloped his horse home from the pasture.

The hound was panting fiercely, but deeply and rhythmically, so intent on catching Skeezix that it paid no attention to Reddy when he pulled past.

Although there was only ten feet of space between the hound and Skeezix, Reddy shot between them, crossing Skeezix out. It was so close that Reddy tucked his tail between his legs as he went through so the greyhound could not seize it.

Instantly, the hounds left Skeezix and swung in behind Reddy, never losing the stride that carried them over the grass in long, graceful sweeps.

It was close. But it was fun. Now it was time for even greater fun. He would show them a grade of running they had never seen. Again he heard the black hound baying. He knew that he would have to devise some way to hide his scent from her.

And then he thought of a way. But he would need to put distance between himself and her to bring it off.

Winding up his tail, Reddy flew. It was as if a gust of wind had come along and blown the coyote like a leaf.

For a mile, he ran strongly, enjoying the pressure of the wind in his face. Behind him, the black hound's bawling grew fainter and fainter.

Ahead, the land lay in long grassy swells, perfect for speeding. For a moment, Reddy pleasured himself. Legs blurring, he accelerated to such full velocity that a rabbit he passed did not have time to flee and only stared at him as he flashed by. He felt no fatigue, only exhilaration, as if he could run like this for hours.

Finally, he ran over a knoll and into the dry sand of an arroyo. He remembered that his mother had taken them into dry sand when they had left the dirt road that morning.

In dry sand, the scent must be poor, Reddy reasoned. He looked back of him. As fast as he ran through it, it caved in behind him, filling his tracks and burying his scent.

Slowing to a lope, he reviewed the incident in his mind and came to several conclusions. He had not liked the pinch of those teeth into his rear leg, nor of being on his back with greyhounds all around him. He and Skeezix had narrowly escaped death.

He sat down in the buffalo grass, tail curled

around his rear paws, and licked the cut in his right rear ham where the black hound had gashed him. There were two kinds of hounds, he had learned.

Trail hounds and sight hounds. Now he knew why his mother had made him and Skeezix lick their feet and run down the road, where there would be no bushes, or weeds, or grass to which their scent might cling.

Whether the pursuing hound bayed was the clue. If it did, it was a trail hound and would follow him relentlessly. Unless he erased his scent, it might discover him no matter how well he was hidden. He would have to broaden his defensive tactics. Now they had to include scheming against smelling dogs, as well as sight-running dogs.

In late afternoon, when the sun was descending through the willows along a wash, throwing long lacy shadows across the low places, Reddy found himself alone in the middle of Buck Karns' big sheep pasture. There, after a day of grazing, broad streams of woolly backs poured slowly down the slopes, pointed toward their bed ground by the intelligent dogs.

That bed ground, and why they had to use it, had made Karns red necked with rage. Having to drive hundreds of sheep each night to a common sleeping space is bad for the stock and bad for the grass. The sheep trample it out before it is eaten.

Driving in the dust takes off most of the weight

the day's grazing has put on. Herders know that sheep should be allowed to scatter while feeding, bedding down wherever night finds them. But on Buck Karns' range that was too dangerous.

Karns was trying desperately to cut his sheep losses to a coyote killer that nobody—not even ranger J. C. Clack—could bring to bay. While other farmers and ranchers had also been hit, Karns had lost twenty-seven lambs to the Wilderness murderer, including Betsy, a pet his children had bottle raised from an orphan.

Karns thought all coyotes killed lambs, but he was wrong. The assassins are usually individual killers and in the Wilderness there was only one.

Reddy finally saw it. Ahead of him, slouching at a half-crouch through a weed clump, moved a yellow coyote, its tail dangling and tangling with its loose-jointed legs. Through slitted eyes, Reddy studied the stranger curiously.

Not as big as Buff, this coyote was focusing on a small group of sheep that had strayed from the main band and was snatching a few final mouthfuls before the herder and his dog drove them to the security of the bedding ground. Once they reached it, they would be safe.

It was obvious to Reddy that the stranger coyote planned to intercept them before this could happen. The trick was to make the kill before the sheep became closely bunched, and as near sundown as possible, so that the victim would not be missed.

From the area of the bed ground came a multitudinous murmuring of *baas,* the barking of the sheep dog, and the distant voice of the herder as the main flock began to come together.

Reddy saw that the stranger coyote had nicely calculated everything. The coyote was downwind from the dog and would probably try to kill when the straggling sheep were out of sight in a draw. Then their protectors would be too far away to know or interfere.

With movements as smooth and deliberate as pouring honey, the yellow coyote began its stalk. Reddy froze on his stomach, stirred by its artistry. Its tail hung low, its chin brushed the ground, and its body melted into every rock, bush, and grass clump along the way.

Ears pricked forward, nose palpitating, eyes fixed intently on the foolish stragglers it had followed so furtively and so far, it advanced as deliberately as a puff of wood smoke on a calm day.

Every few feet, it would slow to a crawl, sinking so flat on its belly that Reddy could see only the tips of its ears, translucent in the late sunshine, swiveling from left to right as they checked out every sound. Then it resumed the stalk.

As it neared the little cluster of sheep, its movements became bolder and swifter, without sacrificing any of its stealth. Then Reddy saw that the stalker was a female.

Like a stone from a slingshot, she dashed among the sheep. Frantic, they scattered in all directions, bleating in mild alarm. But the killer did not miss. Her jaws closed upon the head and jugular of a fat little lamb. Without ever seeing its attacker, the lamb died quickly.

And Reddy sank lower, his head between his paws, thinking. Why kill an animal that big? And yet the flesh of a young sheep might taste most delectable. He decided to stay around and see what happened, being careful to remain outside the other coyote's scent range.

For a moment, the yellow coyote stood with bloody lips beside her kill, ears jabbed forward, eyes searching in all directions, nose asking the air for information about anything that might be unfriendly to her, or to her purpose.

Satisfied, she began to eat, tearing off mouthful after mouthful of the tender meat. With every mouthful, up would go her head to sniff the wind, or listen to what was in it, or make a visual survey. Reddy watched, fascinated.

Once, the coyote left the victim and trotted down a bank to a nearby water hole. There she drank quickly, her fierce eyes constantly peering about.

Her thirst satisfied, she backed out, careful to put

her feet in almost the same tracks she had made going down, and returned again to her kill. Reddy kept watching, impressed with her caution and her skill.

Suddenly, she looked behind her and slunk away a few yards, tail between her legs. Twice she halted to sniff the atmosphere and to look back over her shoulder with anger and disappointment. Then she vanished into the brush.

Reddy thought, when a coyote kills a sheep, it is always in danger. It must eat in a hurry, looking up after every gulp. He licked his lips hungrily. Perhaps the danger was worth the risk. He wondered what had happened to make her leave.

The stink of the automobile's exhaust fumes reached him before the sound of its gently vibrating motor. Buck Karns' blue pickup truck approached, bobbing over the pasture's bumps and terraces. Karns, the big man at the wheel, had always boasted that he could drive that pickup anywhere he could ride a horse. With him was John Selman, his foreman.

From one of his windmills, Buck had been scrutinizing his sheep with his binoculars. He had seen the alarmed behavior of the stragglers and had driven to the spot to investigate, afraid of what he might find.

Then he found it. Yanking his emergency brake, he jerked the truck to a stop, leaving its motor running. Both he and Selman got out, walking rapidly toward the patch of white on the prairie. Reddy flattened himself in the sage a hundred yards above them. They carried no gun. Might have one in the truck, however.

"Looks like another one down, chief," Selman said.

Buck Karns began to swear, quietly and vehemently. "Coyote! I'd like to shoot him through the guts and laugh at him when he snaps at the holes. This sheep's been dead only a little while. Killer probably saw us coming."

Listening from the sage, Reddy could tell from the man's voice, which sounded like an animal growling, that he was mad. And Reddy knew why.

John Selman knelt for a closer look, then squinted up at his employer. "It was probably an old dog coyote. Yesterday I saw one on that red ridge yonder. If I'd had a gun, I'd a got him sure."

Buck Karns sneered. "If you'd had a gun, he'd never have let you seen him."

He stood. Reaching into his shirt pocket, he shook a cigarette out of the pack and lit it, drawing deeply on the first inhalation. His upper lip was curled angrily over his teeth.

John Selman stood and looked at him. "Think we ought to salt the corpse with strychnine?"

Buck Karns' eyes gleamed. "Just as well. He might come back tonight to finish his dinner. Looks like he just got started."

From the blue pickup, they brought a package.

But first Buck Karns sat in the pickup's open doorway, drawing on sheep-pelt moccasins over his boots and pulling on sheep-pelt gloves. Careful not to move the lamb's body, he inserted the poison with a forked stick. Then they left.

From the shoulder of the ridge to which he had retreated, Reddy saw the blue pickup limping over the terraces to the bedding ground.

All night long, the body of the lamb lay on the prairie. Reddy, hidden under a yucca plant two hundred yards above it, was curious to see the incident through to its end.

Two hours before dawn, his patience was rewarded. He heard a yawn, and then the soft intake of a coyote's breath. The yellow female had returned to visit her kill.

Cautiously, she slunk toward it, a foot at a time, until she had approached within fifty yards. Then she did something that Reddy found most incredible.

For the first time, the wind came fair from the dead lamb to her, and she got her first whiff of the man scent. Karns had not thought how pointless it was to disguise his odor by covering his feet and hands when a minute before they had walked to the carcass without any such covering.

The shock of the discovery galvanized her into a contortion that made it seem she might break her back. With a yelp of terror, she leaped straight up. Whirling in midair, she came down on legs as stiff as pokers and went streaking off into the dark.

Dropping to his belly, Reddy tried to analyze her panic. Her kill, touched by man, was hers no more, she seemed to believe. Still it might become his. He had not eaten since noon and he was famished.

With eyes, nose and ears, he explored the ozone, but found nothing threatening. Walking to the carcass, he felt a vague unease. Strange odors lay everywhere.

There were the odors of Buck Karns and John Selman. There was the sheepy odor of the moccasins and the gloves that was not quite the same as that of the dead lamb. And there was a strange new odor. But the pink meat looked most inviting.

Still wary, Reddy trotted back to the top of the hill and stood there, looking vigilantly in all directions. Then he trotted to another hummock and repeated the maneuver, examining the situation from all sides. He returned to the body.

Circling it once, he sniffed it, then pawed it gingerly, fearing a trap. But there was no scent of steel, so there could be no trap. His hunger gnawed at him.

Moving to the flank of the lamb, he tore off a tentative bite and swallowed it. The taste of the young flesh between his teeth made him ravenous. He began to select choice tidbits from the shoulder, where the yellow coyote had been feeding, chewing with juicy greed.

Within a few minutes, Reddy felt excruciating pains in his stomach, then cramps and nausea. The prairie swam before his eyes, dimming them. Toppling over on his side, he began to kick. With the fighting instinct of his breed, he staggered to his feet.

Coyotes instinctively throw up anything that doesn't agree with them. Reddy vomited all the lamb he had eaten. The dark prairie came back into focus and he could see again. He bolted some blades of green grass and felt better.

He did not know it, but Buck Karns, furious at the new depredation, had planted too much strychnine in the body. Had less poison been introduced, Reddy would not have felt the pains until it was too late.

As he lay on his stomach, he admired the yellow coyote. She had smelled the peril from fifty yards away and had fled with a fear that was almost hysterical. He recalled the strange odor of the poison that had disturbed him when he first sniffed at the corpse, etching it permanently into his memory. He never wanted to forget it.

Of one thing he was sure. He had all the fresh lamb he wanted for the rest of his life.

Fun at Fanshaw

As October melted into November and frost began to coat the buffalo grass, Reddy accompanied Skeezix on the latter's excursions of mischief making.

Although Reddy was more cautious than his brother, he quickly became Skeezix's equal at plotting original ways to dupe the dogs or hoodwink the human beings who owned them. Like the day they decided to tantalize Jud Bodkins, the wolfer.

It began a full three hours before daybreak. Both

coyotes had spent half the night in fruitless hunting. They still had not dined when they came upon Bodkins' shack near the old Fanshaw rural school, long since abandoned.

Although the wolfer lived alone, he owned three dozen chickens that the young coyotes longed to prey on. When they called in the daytime and found Bodkins' ancient Ford touring car gone, Caesar, Jud's bulldog, and several mongrel hounds were always there.

And it had been impossible to capture one of the wolfer's fowls at night because they slept high in the branches of the mesquite trees that grew in a sprawl below Bodkins' cottonwood pole barn.

In the dim starlight, the two hungry coyotes studied the situation. A coyote can eat anything, no matter how disgusting. But he prefers fresh meat.

Skeezix went into action. He trotted first to the tree farthest from the house, and standing beneath it, looked upward, his keen mind working. The chickens awakened. They began to chatter softly and uneasily.

Suddenly, Skeezix reared up on his hind legs and sprang toward the tree roost. The fowls clucked in alarm, but only climbed higher.

With Reddy watching thoughtfully from a sitting position, to one side, Skeezix tried each tree in turn. The chickens did not take wing. They just kept climbing higher. Not until Skeezix began to run in big circles entirely around the tree, and then made a dash to the trunk, raising himself on his hind legs and placing his forefeet upon it, did a fowl finally flop downward.

Skeezix was on it in a flash and Reddy joined him in the meal. Soon the hen was in their stomachs and its feathers strewn on the ground. But it was just a small hen and only made the coyotes hungrier.

Now it was Reddy's turn. He trotted under the tree. Again the foolish fowls fluttered their wings and made soft frightened noises. Reddy stared up at them, and they stared down at him.

There are few creatures dumber than a chicken. All they had to do to save their lives was close their eyes. But they didn't know that.

Reddy twisted about, grasped the tip of his tail in his mouth and began to whirl round and round beneath the mesquite. Each time he made a revolution on the ground, the chickens made one with their heads in the tree above as they tried to follow his circling. Skeezix sat off to one side, observing the maneuver.

Soon it bore fruit. A fat hen lost her balance and fell, flailing her wings and squawking in terror. Reddy caught her in the air, bit her through the head, and shared the repast with Skeezix.

But they weren't yet through with Jud Bodkins. Reddy would never forget the stale, unwashed odor of the wolfer. He had encountered it first as a puppy when one of Jud's big, hairy hands had pulled him from the hole near the sandbank where the bodies of his four brothers and sisters were laid out.

He had run onto it again when his mother escorted him on the circuit of the wolfer's traps. Here it was everywhere: on the hasp of the barn gate, on the handle of the feed bucket turned upside down over a corral post, and on the left door and steering wheel of the old touring car parked in the yard.

The coyotes stole close to Jud Bodkins' shack and began to howl, the chopped-up notes of their high-pitched wails tumbling over one another in the autumn night.

It got results. A sleepy growl broke from Caesar and he answered back in kind, his deep bay telling his anger and indignation. Although it was only four o'clock, the roosters in the mesquite trees began to crow noisily. Everything on the place awoke except the master. And then he awakened, too.

In the shack, all the lights came on. The screen squeaked and Jud Bodkins walked out the back door in his long underwear and his sock feet, carrying a rifle.

"Shuddup!" he roared to Caesar. The bulldog thrust his tail between his legs and slunk off.

Jud shook his fist at that part of the darkness he judged the coyote howling had come from.

"I'll be after you tan devils come daylight," he growled. "Me an' Old Bob."

Old Bob was a spotted greyhound that Jud Bodkins had purchased from a coyote hunter living east of Scraggs. The dog had made a reputation in that area. Bodkins was eager to try him out in the Wilderness, a formidable testing ground for any hound.

Reddy and Skeezix did not hear the wolfer's threat. Two hundred yards away, they were running swiftly. In the glint of the kitchen light, they had seen the rifle barrel.

When the sun peeped over the red ridge, Jud Bodkins and two of his cronies were out in a pickup with a hound pack. And with them was Old Bob, who wore a woebegone facial expression, and whose nose was so slender that he could almost have taken a drink of water from a gun barrel.

Still hunting in the area, Reddy and Skeezix saw the pickup enter the Wilderness road. At the same instant, Old Bob saw them and began to whine and yelp. Then Jud Bodkins saw them too.

"There they are!" he yelled, "Old Bob saw 'em! He's got a eagle eye!"

Stomping the foot brake, the pickup's owner tried to stop the car. Jud Bodkins jerked the wire that opened the door of the dog box, releasing the dogs before the truck had completely halted.

"Watch my new pothound!" the wolfer yelled. "He'll run right up that red coyote's back, into his ears, and out of his eyes!"

Reddy had never seen such witless beasts, or such a fouled-up operation. As the dogs sprang from the box, they lost their balance, rolling over and over on the ground. In the dust of the sliding pickup, they regained their feet, but losing their sense of direction, they looked north instead of south and ran away from the coyotes instead of toward them.

All but Old Bob. The new hound soon oriented himself, and spotting the coyotes, gave chase.

As Reddy ran, not at all minding the light load of chicken in his stomach, he listened, but heard no baying. These were sight-running hounds, not trailers. The discovery simplified his response and aroused his imagination.

With Skeezix at his flank, he cut to the right, heading for the rolling country and especially for a narrow ditch he knew about. When he reached it, he lay down in the ditch and whined for Skeezix to join him. In an instant, both were out of sight to the dogs.

Soon they heard the patter of racing feet. The pursuing pack, led by Old Bob, leaped the ditch, crossing directly over them, and passed on over a small hill. As Reddy jumped out of the depression, laughing out of both sides of his mouth, Jud Bodkins and the hunters saw him.

Shouting and swearing, the men recovered their dogs and returned to the scene, trying to sight the coyotes. Reddy bobbed over a rise and halted boldly in the open, just out of range of Jud Bodkins' .22 rifle. Again Old Bob sighted him and the pack gave chase.

For half an hour, Reddy and Skeezix made sport of that pack in the manner that so delights the coyote soul. Again Reddy led them to a ditch, a different one this time, and lying on their backs, he and Skeezix again heard the foot beats and the fierce panting and saw the heads, bellies, and tails of the hounds sweep over them.

Emerging, the coyotes followed the hounds and when the latter, having lost sight of the quarry, began to circle, Skeezix barked mockingly behind them and the chase began all over again with Reddy and Skeezix crossing each other out so many times that they became fagged in the Indian summer heat.

Dogs and coyotes were milling all over the landscape. Finally, Old Bob lost sight of everybody. Disgusted with coyotes who would not respond in the accepted manner, he came trotting back toward the pickup. The rest of the pack was still chasing Reddy while Skeezix rested in a sage clump on a hill.

Although he did not know it, Old Bob was trotting straight toward Reddy and the oncoming hounds. Looking up, he saw what was speeding toward him.

The spotted greyhound gave a peculiar squeal. Turning around, he fled in the opposite direction, ears mashed against his head, tail stuck between his legs in arrant fear. For a moment, it was a strange race.

Old Bob was leading, Reddy ran second, and the hound pack trailed a distant third.

Tiring of the fun, Reddy twirled his tail and skedaddled for home. Behind him, the wolfer and his pals collected the jaded hounds, put them into the dog box, and turned back toward Jud Bodkins' shack to drown their frustration in cheap whiskey.

"Look at Old Bob," taunted one of the wolfer's associates, peering over his shoulder at the spotted hound standing sadly in the coop. "He looks like he's been rode hard and put away wet!"

"I'm gonna take him out in the country an' run away from him," said another.

"I'll sell the so-and-so," vowed Jud Bodkins. "I'll git thet red coyote yet!"

Skeezix, nicely calculating Reddy's intention, cut across the flats and met him at the pond on Sand Creek.

There the ash-colored coyote waded into the water, as Reddy knew he would, and reclined with only his nose showing. Reddy walked to a ledge above and, choosing a spot that commanded a view of half a mile in all directions, lay down in the warm sand. His toes tingled with pleasure. He was laughing with his yellow slanted eyes.

Although the sun was not quite two hours high, it had been a most intoxicating morning.

A month passed. Only a few ivory-colored leaves remained on the cottonwoods along Sand Creek. The buffalo grass was the color of straw. With food becoming scarce, Reddy allowed Skeezix to conduct him one night on a prowl of the garbage cans in the small town of White Bead.

Reddy was nervous. The breaks of the Wilderness ran right up to the outskirts of the sleeping village, and as they glided past the darkened church, Reddy remembered that time he had followed the Peter Zook family to it. He wondered if its occupants still shouted and moaned in unison in the manner that had agitated his ears.

He had never before entered the town itself, with its small wooden houses, each darkened and filled with sleeping people. Reddy could hear their snoring. He could scent them, too, and also their cats and their sleeping dogs.

Smells beyond the scope of his experience kept crowding into his nostrils and making him uneasy: coal smoke from the chimneys of the houses, gasoline fumes from the automobiles parked silently by them, and the sour stench of the garbage kept in large metal cans along the alleys.

After they had dined silently from three cans on a quantity of discarded table scraps, Skeezix headed confidently down the highway east of town. Reddy hung back. The scent of hounds, a great many hounds, was on the wind from that direction. What mischief was this reckless brother of his leading them into now?

Through the starlight, Reddy saw ahead a big dog pen bounded on all sides by chicken wire. In it several hounds were sleeping. Although he sensed that they were confined, he doubted the wisdom of approaching them anyhow.

Skeezix looked back and whined pleadingly. Come on, he seemed to urge. Let's torment them. It will be fun.

Reddy hung back, sinking to his belly. He did not want any of that kind of fun.

Skeezix trotted boldly up to the pen. Obviously, he had been there before. He yipped twice, awakening the dogs. Growling and gnashing their teeth, they crowded against the chicken wire. Reddy was on his feet, ready to fly.

Around and around the pen Skeezix trotted, looking at them as if they were the dirt under his feet. He was prancing on his toes, his puffed-out tail hoisted in disdain. Although he made no sound, his mocking manner spoke volumes.

You couldn't catch us if somebody did turn you out, he seemed to taunt them. You wouldn't have the courage to try. You won't even fight us unless you're six to one.

"Woof! Woof! Woof!" replied the hounds. They

sprang at the wire as if trying to demolish it. Their teeth were clicking with rage. Reddy sank down, head between his forepaws, watching in wonder.

Skeezix trotted off a few steps. Suddenly, he wheeled and charged straight at the dogs in the pen, pretending that he was trying to break into the enclosure. He leaped, letting his thirty-pound body glance lightly off the wire. He landed softly on his feet outside. This infuriated the hounds.

"Boo! Boo! Boo!" they raged and fell to fighting among themselves, biting each other cruelly. With a final look of contempt, Skeezix loped off nonchalantly.

Reddy joined him noiselessly, head pivoting alertly as he probed the air for signs of pursuit. There was none.

Skeezix settled into an unhurried trot, but Reddy felt like flying. The only part of the adventure he had enjoyed was eating the table scraps. He yearned to be back in the Wilderness, where everything was familiar and he was much more sure of himself.

Winter is the coyote's worst enemy, worse even than dogs or man. Food became so scarce in Reddy's first winter that after he and Skeezix had eaten all the persimmons off the ground, they finally ventured across the Cannonball into Peter Zook's north pasture where a grove of blackjack timber relieved the monotony of the prairie.

From a sandy eminence, he saw the Zook home,

whitewashed and friendly, a thin wisp of wood smoke coiling from its chimney into the sky.

For a moment, he thought back upon his babyhood there, and of the little Amish girl who had mothered him so affectionately before he made the change that swung his life into a wilder and more purposeful swirl.

It was a late afternoon in December and the leaves of the blackjacks tinkled like tiny muted bells. The north wind had a bite on it and Reddy felt frisky and playful.

He was walking calmly behind Zook's grazing milk cows, trying to use them as beaters to flush mice out of the tall grass, when Zook, on the buckskin, rode out of the trees, accompanied by Shep, his hound. Surprised, Reddy bolted toward the river.

"Hoooo-eeeee!" Peter Zook called to his hound. "There's a coyote! Go get him, boy!" Shep sprang after Reddy. Spurring the buckskin, Peter Zook cantered after Shep.

Reddy, who saw at once that Zook did not carry a gun, ran toward a barbed wire fence, knowing that he could dart beneath it but that a man on a horse would be halted.

It was good strategy. Peter Zook had to gallop around through an open gate before he could turn down the fence and see the chase. What he saw made him grin with admiration for the coyote.

Reddy flitted down the line of the fence, whipping back and forth beneath the lower wire. He could pass under it faster than Shep, whom he watched carefully over his shoulder. The dog lost ground every time he tried to follow the coyote beneath the barrier.

From the saddle of his running horse, Peter Zook slapped his leg with glee. That coyote knows my fence and my land lots better than me or my dog, he laughed to himself. Those dips and draws are all new to Shep. All he's looking for is the coyote.

Suddenly, Reddy darted beneath the wire, faked to go left, then cut suddenly back to the right.

Trying to cut with him, the dog lost his balance and rolled over and over on his back, whereupon Reddy spun his tail in a bushy circle and vanished into the timber.

Peter Zook pulled up behind a small cedar and stood in his stirrups, frowning thoughtfully. There was no mistaking the coyote's trick of winding up its tail, nor its red color. That's got to be Susy's Scoundrel, he decided.

As he sat there breathing his horse, he got a second surprise. Reddy came trotting back through the trees from a different direction, grinning from ear to ear. The coyote stopped every few feet, watching and listening in the direction in which Shep had disappeared. It was plain to Peter Zook that the coyote was seeking the hound.

Reddy dropped his nose to the ground and moved about. Quickly, he found Shep's scent. He followed it unerringly, tracking the dog into the trees. Peter Zook watched with curiosity and amusement.

After half a minute, a coyote's teasing bark sounded from deep in the timber, followed by a dog's single snarl of rage. The chase was on again, this time because the coyote willed it.

Soon Reddy appeared again. Running swiftly and gracefully, he was skimming over the same course of the fence line, only this time he was reversing it. His grin stretched wider than ever.

Fifty yards behind him, came Shep. Once more, the dog was permitting himself to be led on the fool's errand back and forth beneath the lower wire.

"I chust know it was Susy's coyote," Peter Zook told his family at dinner that night. "*Ach,* how fast he goes! Full sized he is, now, but he still that tail winds up when he gets ready to scat. And his fur is still the color of these old red hills, yet."

Susy listened spellbound, her brown eyes glistening in the soft light of the kerosene lamp. Was it really Reddy that her father had seen?

Jack Dietz

One morning a week later, Skeezix committed an indiscretion that plunged the Wilderness War into an ominous turn for the coyotes.

Always hungry, the ash-colored coyote trotted through the sage to Ranger J. C. Clack's farm adjoining the Wilderness. And Reddy, against his better judgment, trotted with him.

From their hiding place on a sun-warmed slope, where the north wind blew off the farm toward them and they could analyze all its smells, the coyotes examined the situation carefully. The odors were not alarming. Neither were the sights, nor the sounds.

The gray hens with bluish-black striped feathers were cackling merrily from their nests. The concrete swimming pool was drained for winter, its floor covered with leaves and blowing dirt. Clack's hounds were kenneled. The ranger's black pickup truck was gone and both coyotes knew that his wife was afraid to pick up a gun, let alone shoot it.

Skeezix looked at Reddy, whining an invitation.

Reddy dropped his head between his forepaws, and hunkered down in the sage. He still thought that invading a farm in broad daylight was folly.

Skeezix trotted boldly onto the property's buffalo grass lawn, which was now yellowish-gray. He was wagging his tail in the most friendly fashion. Sam, the fierce young German police dog, recognized him and came forward to touch noses. Sam's tail was swinging, too.

When Skeezix pushed over the Clack garbage barrel and the lid came off, making a noise, Reddy looked anxiously toward the house, afraid the woman would hear.

Nobody came to the door. Skeezix began to gulp voraciously from what had spilled out of the barrel. Its smell hung invitingly on the air. Reddy felt his own taste buds contracting and wondered if he had done the right thing staying on the hill.

After Skeezix ate his fill, he and Sam began romping together in the yard, wrestling with each other, chewing each other's neck fur, and nipping at each other's tails with playful growls. From his vantage point in the sage, Reddy nervously scanned the horizon in all directions.

Then Skeezix trotted around to the side of the house. He put his front paws on the outside sill of a window, and rearing up, stared into the kitchen, as if curious to know what the ranger's wife was preparing for dinner. Reddy stood, feeling the hair rising along his back and neck.

His curiosity satisfied, Skeezix joined Sam again in the back yard and they lay down together on the door mat near the concrete back step and went to sleep. And Reddy thought that never in his short life had he seen anything as rash and harebrained as that.

The noise of a racing truck came from the White Bead highway. After receiving the telephone call from his wife, the ranger was hurrying home in his black pickup at seventy miles per hour.

Reddy barked a warning. Skeezix awoke in an instant and flashing out of the yard, joined Reddy in the sage.

J. C. Clack braked the light truck to a stop and

jumped out, a rifle in his hands. But the coyotes ran behind his house and down a wash, where he could not get them in his sights.

When his wife told him about Skeezix standing on his hind legs and peering into the window, Clack sat down and wrote an airmail letter to Washington. He had plenty to do administering his own territory without getting involved trying to exterminate coyotes.

"I've already written to you about the lamb killings that continue on the ranches here," his letter began. "In addition, the coyotes have been knocking over my garbage barrel, making friends with my dog, picking up an odd chicken here and there, and scaring my wife by looking into the kitchen window. I think it time that the Division of Predator Control took a hand."

A week later, Reddy saw the new man at J. C. Clack's home. He was shorter and stockier than Clack. He had bowed legs and an outthrust chin. One of his legs seemed shorter than the other, but in spite of that, his head did not bob up and down when he walked, as did the ranger's.

He seldom walked anyhow, preferring to drive everywhere in an orange pickup truck with a white stripe around its body. At his belt, he wore a pistol in a holster. He kept a rifle in a sheath above the visor of his truck. He slept in the Clack's small guest house.

The man was Jack Dietz, a professional hunter and trapper from the government's Division of Predator Control. "He knows more about killing coyotes than anybody else in the whole division," Clack told Buck Karns.

Dietz's mission was to stop the sheep killing by reducing drastically the Wilderness coyote population. To do this, he would use rifle, trap, and poison, and use them expertly. And he would employ another means, too.

Clack introduced Dietz to the Wilderness farmers at a beef barbecue in his home. The Wilderness men looked with interest at the professional who had come to save their flocks.

Dietz had a round deadpan face that never changed expression. His dark hair, slicked down by brilliantine, was parted in the middle. He seemed somber and aloof, as if he lived in a world all of his own.

His black eyes, wary and distrustful, were hooded and hawklike. When he fastened them on whomever was speaking, he stood still as stone and his stare became so penetrating that the man upon whom it was fixed usually made a mental note to choose his words more carefully thereafter for fear that he might be held accountable for them later.

Few of the farmers liked him. The only time he seemed at all sociable was when the talk shifted to coyote hunting with hounds. Then Dietz's cold eyes lit up. Like everybody else in the country, he felt the same elation over coursing after coyotes that had sent the blood pounding through the veins of the old English squires embarking upon their fox chases.

Next morning, the new arrival was taken on a coyote hunt. It began an hour before dawn. Clack and Dietz went in one pickup, Buck Karns and Frank Thorne in another. It was cloudy and so dark that both Clack and Thorne drove with their lights on. Thorne's pack, most of them trailhounds, was used.

Although he was not invited, Reddy the coyote participated in the hunt. He was digging a ground squirrel from its hibernation hole when Thorne's spotlight pivoted around, revealing him against the skyline. Instantly, Thorne released his hounds.

In the cool hush of early morning, Reddy ran lightly and thoughtfully. Although everything was black, he knew the country so thoroughly that he could almost have run it blindfolded. The wild baying behind him did not worry him.

He resented having his breakfast delayed but his enjoyment of any kind of a race with hounds overshadowed everything. He knew exactly where the ground squirrel had gone underground. He could return for it later.

Because of his hunger, he saw no reason to take the pack into the open areas and waste the hour it would require to run them into the grass. Instead, he scaled a five-foot woven wire fence as neatly as a steeplechaser and led them straight to Milo Briggs' farm. The men followed as closely as possible on the road.

"How come that coyote can see so good in the dark?" asked Thorne. "What keeps him from hittin' trees, bushes, fences, and other things?"

Buck Karns had the answer. "Wolf Thompson says that any varmint born with its eyes shut can see as good at night as by day."

In the other pickup there was also conversation. "That's the reddest coyote I ever saw," said Clack when his headlights caught Reddy's fleeing form crossing the road. "He's red as a strawberry. I think he's the young one Jud Bodkins was talking about. Runs like a streak. Smart as a whip."

On the seat beside him, Jack Dietz grunted contemptuously. "There never was a coyote that couldn't be zapped," he said.

Ahead, Milo Briggs' barns and outbuildings loomed, shadowy and indistinct. Reddy remembered the first race of his life, against Tige Ralston's hounds. He knew that Milo Briggs kept a big pack of house dogs too—shepherds and collies, as well as feists and curs.

He barked twice to let them know he was coming. And what he was bringing. He knew they could hear the trailhounds baying behind him.

A floodlight left on all night illuminated the barnyard. Into its glow, and straight among the wakening house dogs, Reddy led Frank Thorne's pack.

Reddy ran through the house dogs and on into the darkness beyond. But when the hounds tried to follow, the house dogs jumped on them. Instantly, there was growling and snarling. Half a dozen fights raged. The chase was over.

"That danged red coyote knew they'd do that!" stormed Frank Thorne after they had beaten down the dogs and he had got his own hounds back into his pickup.

"Sure he did," said Buck Karns. "House dogs don't like a strange hound pack runnin' through their yard."

Jack Dietz just looked at them scornfully out of his hard eyes, but did not speak. There was a curious, catlike springiness about him even when he sat at ease on a log, a paper cup of hot coffee from Clack's Thermos clutched in one hairy hand.

Later, when Clack drove home, Dietz said, "I'm bringing in my own hounds next week. I've got a portable coop to keep 'em in." He spoke noncommittally, as if the announcement carried no special significance.

When Clack first saw that pack ten days later, his jaw dropped with wonder. They were mostly rough-haired staghounds, deep chested and strong limbed, from Dietz's California ranch. Each dog was a specialist. Wide eyed, Clack listened as Dietz described their duties.

There was a trailhound, a Walker with small yellow spots over his hips. It was his job to scent out the quarry if it could not be seen by the runners. A "jump dog," Dietz called him.

There was a blue female—a Gyp, Dietz called her—with a chest muscled like a wrestler's, legs so long that she appeared to be walking on stilts, and a cold merciless luster in her eyes. Dietz explained that she was a reject, a hotblood, barred from racing on the dog tracks because she fought, as well as beat, the other racers. She was the thrower, or tripper, in Dietz's pack, and also its fastest runner.

Once the coyote was down, one staghound fought the throat, pinning the head so the coyote could not cut or slash. Another grabbed the chest and hung on, trying to break the coyote's ribs. A third, the gut dog, tried to rip open the coyote's stomach.

"Staghounds have more nerve and stamina than greyhounds," said Dietz. "They're tougher, too. They can even trail some. All mine have some chow in 'em. Chow blood gives 'em courage."

But the pack's most awesome figure was Jomo, its killer. Tawny as a lion, he was a crossbred Irish and Russian wolfhound standing thirty inches tall at the shoulder and weighing one hundred thirty pounds. He had a black muzzle and legs which could carry him up to a coyote in a mile's run.

After the reject had thrown the coyote, and the

staghounds had attacked, the killer made his assault
with headlong fury, seizing the victim by the throat or
neck. He had enormous strength and a ferocious
temper. He was ready for a fight, or a kill, at a second's
notice.

The only time Dietz seemed human was when he
talked about his dogs, or was blanketing them after
a trial run, or rubbing them down like racehorses,
or feeding them. The quality of their food astonished
Clack. It was designed to give them extra energy.

In a large kettle outside the wire mesh portable
pen, Dietz kept a dog stew simmering over an open
fire. Big chunks of beef and vegetables had been
cooked down to a rich soup which was thickened by
good graham flour.

Clack smacked his lips. It smelled good enough for
anybody to eat.

They also got buttermilk, bones, and bread in addition to a commercial ration. Dietz fed the pack plenti-
fully the third night after its arrival.

"They'll get very little in the morning," he explained, "because I'm gonna take 'em hunting."

Instead, the hunt came to them. At daybreak,
Dietz was loading them into the dog box of his orange
pickup. The morning had dawned cold and gloomy and
in the wet overcast, the cedars were eternally dripping.
There were other early risers, too.

Reddy and Skeezix, ranging a quarter mile away,

had hunted vainly half the night, catching only a wounded quail that had eluded a hunter crippling it the day before.

Skeezix brought the trouble on himself with his boldness and carelessness. Unable to control his appetite for Mrs. Clack's purebred hens, he disregarded all the strange dog scents and came out of the sage behind the barn. And the Blue Gyp saw him. A good dog is always looking.

With an eager squeal, she leaped out of the pickup, and running through the woodpile, scattered chips right and left as she sprang after him.

"Damn!" yelled Dietz. "There's a coyote!"

Releasing the remainder of his pack, he and Clack ducked inside the cab of the orange pickup. The staghounds flitted across the field like rifle shots through tassels of corn.

Skeezix darted across the Cannonball and headed for the Wilderness breaks three quarters of a mile away. One hundred yards ahead, he should have made it. Reddy was nosing in a grass clump across the highway when Skeezix's running howl of distress pierced the dank air. Rising in pitch, the long cry rang out desperate, quavering.

Instantly, Reddy answered and began running, too. The baying came from his left. He veered across the top of a small ridge, so that he could see better. What he saw wasn't good.

On the flat below, Skeezix was running for his life, pursued by a hound pack and two men in an orange pickup truck. Never before had Reddy seen hounds run as swiftly as these. Each time they humped their backs, they seemed to tread on a hidden spring that, recoiling powerfully, propelled them forward. Driving hard, they seemed determined to end the chase almost before it began.

Skeezix had awakened to a full understanding of his peril. His shaggy coat lay flat in the wind and his shoulders and flanks flexed convulsively. But these silent and terrible antagonists were closing in on him, led by the Blue Gyp who bounded over the prairie like a flat stone skipping across the surface of a pond.

When Skeezix came to a shallow arroyo that turned off behind a small hill, a flicker of hope warmed Reddy's heart.

Skeezix leaped into the arroyo, and turning left, ran down its shallow bed. And this, Reddy saw, was his fatal mistake. The ash-colored coyote was out of sight of the hounds but in the orange pickup Jack Dietz had read the maneuver correctly.

He jerked the light truck to the left, at an angle that would intercept the coyote at the end of the arroyo. He jammed the flat of one hand down on the pickup's horn. The noise echoed weirdly off the surrounding bluffs.

Instantly, the reject from the dog tracks and the

staghounds, too, turned at the summons. Noting the new angle their master's vehicle was taking, they cut across too. Reddy was filled with shock and a sense of futility. This man got right into the hunt with his dogs.

Too far away to help, he could only race alongside and look. He never forgot what he saw.

When Skeezix jumped out of the end of the arroyo, the hounds were literally on top of him. The drama ended in an explosion of red dust only a half a mile from where the chase had begun.

The Blue Gyp sprang, grasped Skeezix's hind leg in her mouth, and capsized him. Skeezix tore loose, and baring his teeth, awaited the final terror, his face flooded with fear. Dietz's team—neck dog, chest dog, belly dog, and killer—moved in. And suddenly Skeezix was on his back and covered with hounds.

In twenty seconds it was all over and the California dogs were wiping the blood off their muzzles on the buffalo grass. And Reddy felt a sudden chill.

Wheeling, he fled into the sage.

Tire Chain and Turkey Bell

After a week, Reddy no longer missed Skeezix. Tragedy is a fact of life that all wild creatures must accept. They fill their bellies by violence. And they die by violence, too.

Regardless of who died, the living had to eat and Reddy was always hungry. But he knew that he had to be cautious.

He distrusted Jack Dietz more than ever. His dread of the professional grew when the orange pickup began to appear more often in the Wilderness. Along the pattern of its tire tracks, Reddy began to find wild game—usually a dead rabbit, a possum, or a road-runner. Remembering the lamb in Buck Karns' pasture, he became even more uneasy.

He did not gobble the bait despite the fact he could detect no scent of human hands upon it. But other coyotes did, and the crows feasted from the bodies lashed to the farmers' fences.

Gradually, some of the coyote sources of food began to disappear. The prairie dog town was mysteriously depopulated. Mrs. Clack's chickens, and those of other Wilderness farms, were carefully yarded at night. Ranchers who owned sheep tightened their custody of the flocks. And Jack Dietz's traps and poisoned baits made such fearful havoc among the Wilderness coyotes that only the strongest and smartest survived.

With Skeezix dead, Reddy began to hunt with his father and mother. It was Buff who taught him how to catch the black-tailed jackrabbits that chewed the corn and ate the wheat. Only Reddy and the Texas coyote could run them down in the open and sometimes it took a dash of miles to do that.

There was an easier way. It was late February and the days were growing longer. On an afternoon of freezing cold, they flushed a big jackrabbit. Ears jauntily erect, it bounded over a rise ahead of them.

Reddy gave instant chase but Buff, whining, ran off to one side, around a hill, and squatted on his haunches.

As usual, Reddy was thinking as he ran. Why had his father refused the race that Reddy always found so fascinating?

Cruising in ten-foot leaps, the big jack gradually began to circle to the left. Soon he was headed back in the direction he had started from, the direction that led to his burrow. Then Reddy guessed his father's motive.

Reddy accelerated so he would be close enough to see the finish. As they raced back, and Reddy began to gain, the big jack's ears were flattened out. He was going his best.

Unknown to him, he was going straight to his doom. Back near the starting point, Buff crouched close to the ground, raising his head slowly above the sage to see the oncoming bunny, then lowering it again and crawling on his belly until he had put himself squarely in its path.

Reddy saw the climax. At exactly the right moment, Buff sprang out of the sage and speared the hare with one swoop of his jaws. Then he and Reddy divided the dinner.

March arrived. The weather seemed unable to make up its mind. One day, the meadowlarks would be singing sweetly from the fence posts. Then the dust would roll in from the northwest, suffocating everything.

Shutting out the sun, the dust made the sand plum scrub and their adornments of white blossoms look like grotesque animals crouching by the roadside. And Reddy, now eleven months old, could taste the dirt in his mouth, and feel it in his fur and between the toes of his feet.

March was also a time for ploughing. On a dusty afternoon in Peter Zook's south field, Reddy learned to use the plough as a means of survival.

While following a porcupine, he was jumped by Wolf Thompson's hounds, the best in the Wilderness before the coming of Jack Dietz's California pack.

Exploding into action, Reddy distanced them but he could not discourage Moonshine, Thompson's best dog. Moonshine, a fawn-colored trailhound with a mellow alto voice that was known all over the White Bead territory, was a very determined dog, and determination is the quality hound owners prize the most. He never wanted to quit a trail.

But like many perfectionists, he had one fault. Every time he gave tongue on a chase, he would stop, turn partly around, throw his head back, and yowl his music as if he was proud of it and wanted everybody behind him to have the privilege of hearing it too. Of course, he always lost ground when he did this.

No matter if he did fall a little behind, Moonshine never quit. Thompson's greyhounds stayed with him, knowing that the coyote would eventually show himself or be flushed.

For two hours, Reddy had played the fugitive, doubling back upon himself or turning on his speed and running off from his pursuers. But behind him he usually left his trail.

He was resting in a hole under a creekside cottonwood when he heard Moonshine's deep-tongued bay four hundred yards behind him.

"Ar-umph—ar-ooooooo!" it sounded. To Reddy, that said, "You can't shake me off. I'm still after you. And I'm going to get you, too."

Flashing to his feet, Reddy ran westward, onto Peter Zook's farm. As he paused at the west creek, lapping up the cool water, he searched his mind for a way to hide his trail.

Ahead of him, Peter Zook was driving a tractor and pulling a three-bottom breaking plow that turned up a strip of moist dirt four feet wide. An idea clicked in Reddy's agile brain.

Although Susy's father was a man and suspicion of all men is a coyote's inborn trait, Reddy knew this man and sensed that he was harmless. He saw that he did not have a gun.

The coyote boldly trotted up the field ahead of the tractor, staying in the unploughed section that in half a

minute would be ripped up by the plough blades, covering his trail.

While the plough was obliterating sixty yards of
his tracks, Reddy whipped down a draw and vanished
into the willows along the river.

In a short time, Thompson's pack, led by the per-
sistent Moonshine, came panting up. When Reddy's
trail, erased by the plough, broke off under Moonshine's nose, the fawn-colored hound sat down, turned
halfway around and his voice, mournful and frustrated,
rang out like a deep-toned church bell. The greyhounds
with him plopped down in the dust, resigned. They
were used to his intonations and had learned to ignore
them.

Wolf Thompson came running up barefooted. He
was gasping for breath. "You seen a coyote come this
way?" he asked.

Peter Zook nodded gravely.

"Which way did he go?"

Peter Zook's small mouth spread into a little smile
that seemed out of proportion to his big face. It showed
his white teeth.

"This coyote I like," he said. "My daughter had
him for a pet once. I want him to live so he can catch
the rodents that eat my crops."

Wolf Thompson looked shrewdly at the strip of
fresh-turned dirt. "He's a wise 'un. I bet he came here
on purpose. I bet he came here so's your plough would

dig up his trail an' my hounds would have nothin' to scent."

Peter Zook nodded. "He's been run so much that he's smart as a human, yet."

"I'm sorry we trespassed on you," said Wolf Thompson. "My dogs was jest follerin' the coyote."

Peter Zook turned off his tractor motor and produced a Thermos and two paper cups. Wolf Thompson wiped his hands on his blue overalls and gratefully accepted the hot coffee that had been freshly ground that morning by the little mill in Rebecca Zook's kitchen.

Peter Zook looked at Moonshine. "I like to hear that hound bawl."

Wolf Thompson snorted. "That's his trouble. He likes to hear hisself bawl."

Next morning, Wolf Thompson told the story of Reddy's trickery up and down White Bead's Main Street. Frank Thorne told it to Buck Karns. And Buck Karns told it to Jack Dietz.

Dietz just sneered. "There never was a coyote that couldn't be zapped," he said. "Time's runnin' out for that coppery one."

It ran out first for another of Reddy's family. It was May now. Invigorated by rain, the buffalo grass rippled in waves of velvety green. Mice and ground squirrels were moving and the chalky sage teemed with infant rabbits. Food was plentiful again.

A new generation of baby coyotes had been born. Reddy saw that Smoky had settled her new brood in the same abandoned badger hole where she had suckled him. Buff did the hunting for them all.

On a sunny afternoon when the pups were five weeks old, nearly ready to wean, Jack Dietz's orange pickup came bouncing over the Wilderness floor. Reddy flattened himself, stiffening with hate. There was no dog box in the pickup bed, but he knew that both a pistol and rifle were always within Dietz's reach.

Half an hour after Dietz passed from view, Smoky's call of distress, a long, quavering cry, pealed out over the Wilderness. Reddy got to her quickly, but Buff was there ahead of him. They found her in a weed patch near an oil slush road.

On her left hind foot was a light steel trap, fastened to an iron drag. It had been substituted for the heavier trap that had caught her. And around her neck hung a leather collar to which was attached a turkey bell, such as farm women use to make turkey hens lead them to their nests in the woods.

Jack Dietz's tracks and scent were everywhere. Through his field glass, he had seen that Smoky liked to walk in a certain portion of an oil slush road so that her scent would be hard to follow. On one side of the road he had concealed a trap. She had not been able to scent it because of the heavy odor of the oil.

After encumbering Smoky with the second trap

and the bell, Dietz had released her, so that when she returned to her den to care for her young, he could trail her there by the marks of the drag and the sound of the bell. Then he would find the pups and destroy them.

For most of the afternoon, Reddy and Buff stayed with Smoky. She had learned to make slow progress by grasping the drag in her mouth and carrying it while she hobbled on three legs pulling the trap. But she couldn't do anything about that bell. Only when she crouched and lay still did it cease its diabolical ringing.

That night, Buff brought her dinner, a half-grown cottontail. She bolted it hungrily, then lay full length in the sage easing the tension on the trap and lessening the pain. Reddy lay in the grass, watching them.

Buff stood over her. He looked back over his shoulder toward the den, whining persuasively. Why don't you go to the den and nurse the pups? he seemed to be asking. But Smoky ignored him.

Next morning, Dietz's orange truck came limping over the Wilderness sward. Parking at the spot where he had trapped Smoky, the government hunter got out. He began following the marks of the drag.

After a walk of half a mile, he found her. She was cowering in a thicket of skin oak, shaking the turkey bell and barking faintly to decoy him away from her family in the den.

Dietz saw the remains of the rabbit Buff had brought her. He decided to try a little longer.

Guessing that she was carrying the drag in her teeth, he took it off, substituting an automobile tire chain. He drove away, figuring that she would surely return to the den to suckle her whelps.

Smoky refused to betray her family. And Reddy quieted the telltale bell by chewing the leather collar in two, the bell dropping harmlessly in the grass.

Buff kept feeding her. Then he began feeding the pups, too, after first chewing and predigesting the rabbit meat he caught, then regurgitating it for them. He was kept very busy. Finally, he moved the pups to another den three miles away.

To do that, he had to travel more than forty miles. There were seven of the furry little creatures and he had to carry them one at a time by the scruff of their necks in his mouth.

Reddy wanted to help him, but Buff snarled, showing his teeth. It was obvious that he regarded it solely as a father's duty.

On the fifth night, Buff and Reddy visited Smoky once more, bringing her a ground squirrel. A spring rain lashed their faces with cold gusts.

Buff looked at the tire chain. It was a deadly, fatal thing, and all three of them knew it.

Buff walked up to Smoky. Intelligent animals are more aware of feelings and emotion than is realized. They touched noses. Then Buff lay down beside her and stayed most of the night, despite the rain.

Next morning, Dietz returned. On a leash in the front seat with him sat the trailhound with the yellow spots on his hips. Buff's tracks, less distinct in the rain, still lay everywhere.

Using the trailhound, Dietz followed Buff's tracks back to the first den. But when he dug it out, it was empty. The pups, and the father, were gone.

Muttering to himself, Dietz tossed the shovel into the bed of his pickup. He put the hound in the cab. The marks of the tire chain were plain. He pulled his rifle from the scabbard and began walking, following the imprint of the dragging chain.

He was satisfied, now, that this coyote mother would never disclose the hiding place of her babies.

Dietz found her in a sumac clump, unable to move. The tire chain had caught on a root, holding her prisoner. For a moment, Smoky's green eyes bored defiantly into his.

The roar of the rifle echoed off the river sand hills.

Death of a Notable

In July, the sun fried the prairie. Long cracks seamed the red earth. The birds had lost all interest in singing and spent much of their time in whatever shade they could find, beaks open, wings trailing. Cicadas chirred maddeningly in the dog-day heat.

Reddy's mother had shown him the previous year how to get some relief. Selecting a high spot so that he could see, he scratched out shallow beds around a sage clump. In the forenoon, he lay under the west side of the sage. At noon, he lay on the north side. In the afternoon, he shifted to the east side. Thus he was always cooled by the shade.

But no matter where he lay, he was tormented by an intolerable thirst. All the water had dried up. No rain had fallen for weeks.

Reddy wanted a drink so badly that he considered stealing a few swallows from Ranger Clack's concrete swimming pool. Then he remembered what had happened to Skeezix and abandoned the idea.

One late afternoon when the low-flying hawks began to feed, the Texas coyote came trotting up to Reddy. His coat, usually pale orange, had taken on the color of brown adobe dust. He looked lean and fit.

Reddy stood, stretching first one hind leg behind him, then the other. Despite his thirst, he had to eat. He envied the Texas coyote. Apparently, he could go for days without water. Reddy had never seen him drink.

Today the Texas coyote was thirsty, too. Just as he had once shown Reddy how to catch snakes during a time of excessive hunger, he now taught him how to find water in a land where everything was as dry as last year's cornstalks.

After trotting half a mile, he halted at a spot near a dry wash. With the sun beating down mercilessly on him, he began to sniff the ground. Reddy sniffed it, too, and detected a very faint odor of moisture. But who could drink an odor?

With his front feet, the Texas coyote began to paw the ground. He made the dry sand fly, pulling it beneath his stomach. Puzzled, Reddy watched, his head held on one side.

When the pile of sand under him grew large, the Texas coyote switched to the opposite side of the hole and began scooping the sand out from that direction.

The sand now looked damp. Mud appeared on the other coyote's feet. He dug some more. Jamming his muzzle into the bottom of the hole, he began to suck and to swallow until soon his thirst was satisfied.

Reddy could not believe it until he had thrust his own nose into the opening and drunk his fill of the cool water. It tasted sweet.

Reddy also hunted with Buff, helping him catch the rabbits that his father bore dutifully to the three pups he now fed at such labor. The other four had died, victims of Jack Dietz's poison pellets.

In late August, the Old One left his lair on a secluded gypsum knoll where no scent would hang, and he and Reddy raided the last of the farmers' watermelon fields.

Better than any other coyote, the Old One knew where to find fruit—wild blackberries, wild grapes, mesquite beans, and the juicy pulp of the cactus. Although the wild plums had frozen and did not bear, he occasionally escorted Reddy on a nocturnal raid of Milo Briggs' apple orchard, and they feasted on the windfalls there.

Summer merged into fall. Everything was yellow now: sunflowers, goldenrod, butterflies, even the big buses that hauled the children to the school at White Bead. Reddy knew what fall meant—hounds, pickups, and men combing the Wilderness for the coyotes that had survived Jack Dietz's summer extermination program.

Dietz hadn't missed very many. A hard worker, he knew coyotes and their habits. His rifle, trap lines, and poisoning took a fearful toll of the pups who were most vulnerable at this stage of their lives.

He had dispatched so many that only the smart ones were left and he felt he could now concentrate on those who for years had deviled the farmers and ranchers and were the subjects of their conversations on the streets of White Bead, or while coffee was being drunk over campfires up and down Sand Creek.

The three they talked most about were Old Social Security, as the Old One was known; Three Toes, a big fellow who ranged east of White Bead; and Reddy, whose speed and cleverness ahead of the hounds was fast becoming a Wilderness legend despite the fact that he was the youngest of them all.

Proud and disdainful, Dietz felt that all this public

adulation of coyotes reflected on him and his program. Unless he slew these coyote notables everybody gossiped about, he could not face the farmers on the streets.

The lamb slaughter had slacked off. Dietz was working hard on that, too. From Buck Karns' and Frank Thorne's back porches, he glassed the country with his binoculars. The yellow coyote would slip along an irrigation lateral, pounce upon a sheep, and drag it from sight so quickly that Dietz could not discover her. But he kept trying to find the sheep killer. He knew there was only one.

On the first frosty morning of the autumn, Reddy yawned. Curling his body down, he began licking the cold white crystals from between his foot pads. He was staring into the shadows with his sly, inscrutable eyes when he heard the coyote howl for help.

Instantly, he was in motion, sprinting to the scene so that he could cross out the animal in trouble, if it needed helping.

When he got there and saw the orange pickup, and the staghounds cavorting around Dietz and sniffing at the small coyote carcass the government hunter easily hefted in one hand, Reddy knew that he was much too late. Crouching in the sage, he watched the man and dogs who were his mortal enemies.

After their triumphant procession had passed

from view, the dead coyote strung head down from the top of the pickup's hound box, Reddy went painstakingly over every foot of the ground, reconstructing the chase from the marks and the scents still hot on the face of the prairie.

There was a familiar scent among them. With a stiffening of his forefeet, Reddy recognized it instantly. Although the small body Dietz had lifted was chewed and bloodied beyond all recognition, its scent clung unmistakably to the grass, the weeds and the skunk brush. It was the scent of the Texas coyote.

Soon Reddy knew what had happened as certainly as if he himself had seen the fatal race. Nosing in the grass, he sniffed the ground. His companion had run well but they had caught him after a chase of three-fourths of a mile. The Blue Gyp had overtaken and thrown him.

Reddy knew it was she because he had memorized her scent when he had examined the ground after they had overhauled Skeezix. The Texas coyote had jerked away from her when she spilled him the first time. Reddy could see it and smell it in the torn turf.

But she had overtaken him a second time and nailed him solidly. And the staghounds, coming up fast, had finished him off, helped by Jomo, the gloomy executioner.

How could they catch him so quickly? Reddy

wondered. The Texas coyote could run almost as fast as Reddy. And he ran a good route. Perhaps they had flushed him from point-blank range.

With his gliding, noiseless gait, Reddy started to trot off, then changed his mind. He half turned, looking nervously across the prairie in the direction the orange pickup had disappeared. Would they catch him, too?

Then pride in his own running prowess surged through him. Nothing on four feet could catch him. But he knew that the day was coming when Dietz's pack would try.

It came sooner than he thought. A little before sundown on a Thursday in November, Reddy was hunting mice in Charley Huff's pasture with one of Smoky's pups. He had seen a lot of his newest brothers and also the six-month-old sister with whom he hunted now. Like Smoky, her fur was the color of pale yellowish smudge.

The bay of Jack Dietz's trailhound surprised Reddy. He knew it was Dietz's Walker because he recognized its high hysterical voice. But he was still surprised because he knew that this wasn't Saturday, the day the hunters were always out in force. He had scouted Tige Ralston's farm that morning and had seen Ralston drive off in his yellow bus.

Heading for familiar territory, Reddy quickly crossed out his sister, whose trail the Walker was following. Then he whipped across the White Bead highway and into the Wilderness, drawing them off her and saving her life. This was all open country and he knew that the rest of the pack had sighted him.

Casting a quick look over his shoulder, he saw them coming through a maize field, led by the Blue Gyp. Dietz's orange pickup was parked along the section line road. Clack was with him.

Dietz thrust his high-powered rifle through the open left door panel, leveling down on the fleeing coyote. Then his face hardened in cold fury and he sheathed the weapon.

Clack, the ranger, looked at him with surprise, wondering why he had not fired.

Quickly distancing the Walker, the staghounds straightened out and began swallowing the ground in long leaps.

Accepting the challenge, Reddy swung his tail in a quick revolution and broke down a fence line, the posts coming back to him at high speed. His body felt tuned for running. And the route seemed especially familiar.

Then he recognized it. It was roughly over this same course that Skeezix had run that fateful morning when this same pack had overhauled and killed him.

Reddy remembered how Skeezix had cut to his left down an arroyo, out of sight of the dogs but not of Dietz who had jerked his pickup to the left and honked his horn, signaling his hounds to cut across with him.

A powerful temptation seized Reddy. He would not shame this pack with all-out running. This man and his dogs were thinking about the other chase. It would be great fun to fool them.

Reddy headed for the spot where Skeezix had entered the gully. Slackening his pace to be sure they saw him, he turned left, darting down the gully.

The noisy blast of Dietz's horn elated Reddy. He knew that all of them—dogs, men, the orange pickup— were cutting across. He waited an instant, then while he was out of sight to them, he turned around and ran back over his own footsteps in the direction from which he had come.

Ahead, he saw a sloping cottonwood tree, a giant that had been struck and felled by lightning. Reddy leaped to its trunk and ran along it for a distance. Then he jumped off it into a cutbank of dry sand and fled up the arroyo to freedom.

At the opposite end of the arroyo, Dietz's staghounds, looking baffled and shamefaced, milled in circles as they scanned the horizon for the coyote who had vanished as if snatched from the prairie by a helicopter.

Whining, the Blue Gyp did the sagacious thing, running to the top of a small hill to examine the countryside. But Reddy stayed out of sight.

Dietz was calling for the Walker. Putting a chain

leash on him, he took him back to the place where Reddy had entered the arroyo.

The coyote's trail was still hot. The trailhound followed it to where Reddy had turned around. The dog stopped, circling aimlessly. Dietz saw in the sand the faint impression of Reddy's return tracks and started the Walker backtracking. The trailhound led them to the cottonwood, then stopped, snuffling the ground and baying excitedly.

"Shut up!" snapped Dietz. "You're telling him we're coming."

"I'll bet he jumped on that cottonwood log," said Clack.

"Naw!" growled Dietz, "he's not that smart."

Finally, Dietz found the place where Reddy had indeed leaped off the trunk. He started the Walker on Reddy's new trail. But Reddy, expecting them, ran down the middle of a shallow creek where the water was rose colored because of the red sand bottom. The Walker could not scent him in the water.

As Dietz and Clack walked the pack back to the pickup, they met Wolf Thompson and three of his hounds. As usual, Wolf was as barefoot as his dogs.

While Clack told him what had happened, Dietz stood silent, his black eyes glowering. He wished that Clack wasn't so gossipy. He hated to be outdone by any varmint. Now the whole town of White Bead would know how this one had tricked him.

Wolf Thompson looked at Dietz and grinned. "I know what happened, captain," he said. "Back there in that arroyo, that coyote stopped to read his road map. It told him to turn around and run in the other direction. So there he ran. A coyote, captain, don't run wild. He always reads his road map."

Clack looked faintly amused. "Maybe so," he said, "but crossing on that cottonwood was the coyote's own idea. He didn't read that on any road map."

As Dietz and Clack drove home in the twilight, Clack used the pickup's lighter to ignite his cigarette. Then he looked at Dietz.

"When your dogs first jumped him, and you had your rifle on him, why didn't you pull the trigger? You had a good shot at him, several in fact."

Eyes blazing, Dietz spat out the open window. "I recognized him and decided not to," he muttered. "I'm gonna beat that one at the thing he does best—running."

After that, the Wilderness war raged with the fury of a final struggle. And it became mainly a duel between Dietz, the crack government professional, and Reddy, the coyote who had wrung so much wisdom from the land and its challenges. "That coyote can't be just two years old," Wolf Thompson protested. "Nobody ever learned all the things he knows in two years."

It was Dietz who swallowed his pride and orga-

nized by rural telephone the master hunt early in
December.

Eight pickups, a driver and companion in the
front seat of each and a box full of hounds in the rear
met at Buck Karns' ranch two hours before sunup for
a breakfast of sausages, buckwheat cakes, and coffee
strong enough to float an iron wedge. Most of the talk
was about coyotes.

"The further up the creek you go, the worse they
get, an' I come from the head of it," boomed out Joe
Griffin, a big lantern-jawed man who had driven his
pack fifteen miles in a cream-colored pickup to make
this hunt.

There was lots of laughter and good-natured
banter, some of it directed at Dietz.

"You think that red coyote's gonna cooperate this
time, captain, and cut across when you do?" asked
Wolf Thompson. Everybody snickered. A fearless little
man, Wolf Thompson would not have been afraid to
poke fun at the devil himself.

"You been teachin' your dogs how to walk a cottonwood log, Dietz?" added Tige Ralston.

Dietz didn't like it, but he took it, managing a
grin. His black eyes lit up scornfully. They were jealous
of his pack. He'd show them yet.

"Old Social Security knows we're comin' after
him," vowed Frank Thorne. "Last night I got him in my

field glass over near Fanshaw. He was standin' on his hind legs with one ear glued to a telephone pole. He was listenin' in, monitoring our plans."

Milo Briggs' round face creased in a smile. "He goes to the highways every time I chase him," he said. "He knows that dogs ain't got no sense crossin' a road. But who ever heard of a coyote gettin' killed by a car?"

"He always heads for Interstate 40 when I'm after him," said Wolf Thompson, and again the laughter rang out, loud and hearty.

Dietz drained his coffee and stood. He was tired of all the levity.

"Les go," he said, and a dozen chairs scraped back. He had a special reason for wanting to get started.

With his field glass the day before, Dietz had discovered Reddy's lair in the sage at the top of a ridge. But he kept the information hidden behind his hooded eyes. He intended to start hunting there. If possible, he hoped to flush Reddy early and cut him off from the badlands, making him run across the flats.

In the Wilderness, the yellowish-gray tint of the buffalo grass was just becoming discernible in the pale light of dawn when Dietz heard the Blue Gyp's sudden yelp of discovery. With a jerk of the wire behind him, he freed all his hounds except Jomo, the anchor dog, whom he kept in a separate compartment.

They hit the frosty turf running, leaving behind

them the smell of scented weeds bruised by their flying feet. Squinting through the thin atmosphere, Dietz saw the coyote, ears canted forward, bounding coolly over the frozen ground in a distant wheat field. That it was a quarter mile away did not worry Dietz in the slightest. His pets could run miles, if necessary.

Spinning the steering wheel of the orange pickup and entering the Wilderness, he hoped with all his heart that it was Reddy.

But it wasn't. And not until the gaunt fugitive had crossed and recrossed the White Bead highway half a dozen times in the first mile of the race did Clack, frowning thoughtfully in the seat beside Dietz, guess the coyote's identity.

"I think that's the old man," he said, face puckering shrewdly. "Old Social Security, they call him. He never lets you get a close turnout on him. And he likes to go to the roads."

Black eyes flashing with elation, Dietz increased the pickup's speed and thought about it. Old Social Security was a celebrity, too, famous for his stamina and his guile. For years, he had outsmarted the best hounds in the Wilderness, tying his trail into a knot, then melting before them like the dewdrops on the yucca growing along the way.

The drivers of the other pickups, honoring Dietz's pack and keeping their own hounds confined in their dog boxes, also recognized the coyote graybeard. They were talking excitedly to one another on the shortwave radios with which each truck was equipped.

"That's Old Rusty-Fusty himself," said Milo Briggs. "Runs in a straight line. Never wastes a step."

"He's headin' west!" Lige Lancaster's exultant voice crackled amid the static.

"He's figurin' on crossin' the state line into Texas," croaked Wolf Thompson. "He knows Texas don't pay no bounty fer coyote ears."

"Then he'd better cross it quick," said Charley Huff. "Dietz's hounds are eatin' him up."

After the chase had gone two miles, the Old One tried for the cover of a canyon. Ditez raced the orange pickup recklessly around the hounds to cut him off, turning him into the open again. It was definitely not a sporting gesture, but nobody in a coyote chase is interested in sportsmanship or rules.

After that, the Old One seemed to hunch his shoulders resignedly, and to lengthen his stride, as if reconciled that this would be another of the long hard races he had never lost.

Reddy the coyote was running, too, as he followed the action from the ridge, hoping to cross out his old friend if the opportunity arose. He had heard the roaring of the pickups and the chatter of their shortwave radios as they filled the section line roads trying to keep the race in sight.

From half a mile away, the race looked to Reddy

like a thread with eight knots in it being slowly pulled across the landscape. Dietz's hounds, bounding fiendishly over the prairie, had cut the Old One's lead to seventy-five yards.

As Reddy ran, he studied his friend's tactics. The Old One could think in action, devising a plan in the back of his hoary head. He would need that plan quickly because the Blue Gyp was now only fifty yards back. And then, the Old One's strategy was suddenly revealed.

Ahead of him in a small pasture, several big brown mules stood in the lemon light of dawn, like long-eared ghosts.

The Old One knew these mules and they knew him. When he ran fearlessly among them, they did little else than cock their long ears and look at him with eyes as mild as a fawn's.

When the Blue Gyp dashed among them, trying to follow the coyote, the mules snorted piercingly. Lowering their heads, they attacked her and the other hounds, braying and biting, and throwing up their heels. The Old One scurried into a culvert.

Dietz was watching and saw him. He stepped across the road for a bundle of alfalfa with which to block one end of the culvert.

The Old One, peeking out of the culvert, saw what Dietz was up to and shot out the other end. And when Dietz finally got his pack to see the running

coyote, the race resumed with the Old One again four hundred yards ahead.

Invigorated by his rest, he ran three more miles before the Blue Gyp threw him in a patch of soilbank grass.

Turning, he swung his body halfway up in a final marvel of litheness, and white teeth shining, snapped viciously and desperately at her. Then the snarling staghounds closed in, joined by Jomo the killer.

In another minute, the Old One was a dead legend instead of a live one. And the hounds were refreshing themselves by standing or lying in a little prairie pool, panting violently.

All but the Blue Gyp. Even with the victim prone and senseless, she kept leaping in to seize him by the throat and shake him, as if loathe to give up the fight.

Reddy watched it all from a shock of corn in a nearby field. Soon there were other spectators. One after another, the pickups arrived—blue ones, brown ones, red ones, yellow ones—debouching the farmers and the ranchers.

All of them crowded up at close range to see in death the notorious figure they had failed to subdue in life. The Old One lay quietly, teeth bared in a final snarl. He had run himself into such exhaustion that his legs were stiff as steel pegs.

Dietz carried him into the middle of the road, propped him up on his feet, and stepped back grinning.

To everybody's amazement, the coyote's legs were still so rigid that he stood alone, his head flopped down unnaturally on his matted chest. Although he was dead, he looked alive. The roar of laughter that went up carried to the young coyote concealed behind the shock of corn.

An automobile drove up and stopped. Its driver, Mrs. Satterfield, the lady mail carrier, was on her way to the post office at White Bead. She saw the coyote standing in the road. She leaned out, looking perplexed.

"What's the matter?" she called. "Won't your dogs kill that coyote?" And the masculine laughter boomed out afresh.

Reddy, crouching in the corn, was saddened by the loss of his friend. He dropped his head between his front paws, his green eyes darting vigilantly at all his enemies—dogs and men—standing triumphantly around the pickups.

They wouldn't catch him. Nothing on four feet could catch him.

Gracey

In winter, when the sumac was stripped of everything but its wine-dark cones and clouds hid much of the sun by day and the moon by night, food became almost nonexistent. After a week of slim gleanings behind the famine, Reddy's appetite was voracious.

In George Boston's pasture, he was chasing a roadrunner which can fly only short distances. He was following it from one sage bush to another, making it fly repeatedly and tiring it, when something flashed in from his left and speared the bird just as it launched itself in flight.

The meddler was a young female coyote. Poised to flee, she looked at Reddy over her shoulder, her mouth so full of the roadrunner that its head hung from one side of her jaws and its tail from the other.

Displeased at losing the breakfast he had followed half a mile, Reddy settled back on his haunches and looked at her. Her movements were quick and neat. She had a small head and small teeth. But no matter how attractive she looked, an empty belly felt the same.

Sitting down, she began to eat, dismembering the bird swiftly and precisely while she watched Reddy carefully out of the corners of her eyes. Dun colored, she had a dark stripe down her back. Like Reddy, she was thin flanked from hunger.

When she had finished, leaving only bits of the skin, feathers and feet, she trotted off a short way and lay down, licking her lips. Her green eyes scrutinized Reddy keenly.

Reddy trotted slowly to the leavings of her meal. He sniffed at them and picked at the little that remained. He was still famished. In the past three days he had dined only on a single field mouse. His lip still hurt where it had bitten him just before he took its life.

He looked at her, his head tilted to one side, his big ears pointed slightly forward. She interested him.

She had clean lines. He decided to be friendly.

Throwing up his head in the movement that invited play, he trotted toward her. With a wonderfully speedy motion, she sprang backward from her prone position, scattering leaves and sticks. Then she wheeled and ran in circles, and although Reddy called upon all his quickness and mobility, he could not catch her.

Suddenly, she crouched, fluffing her fur until she looked like the velveteen pin cushion Reddy had once seen in Rebecca Zook's parlor. Poking her nose within an inch of his, she kept him at bay, as if unwilling to permit any familiarity until she knew him better.

Reddy reared up, sparring at her with his front feet, and the play resumed. With a series of short yelps, he rushed at her and soon they were charging and retreating like dogs enjoying a romp, holding their tails under their bellies, and keeping their front feet out of each other's reach as they scrambled back and forth.

Afterward, a cold wind freshened and it snowed an inch. Lying together for warmth, they spent the day on the south side of a low hill, heads and feet tucked into their bellies and their brushes covering their faces and the backs of their necks.

To Reddy, it seemed a safe place. With the north wind blowing, he knew that their tracks on the opposite side of the hill, where they had come up and over, would soon drift full of snow and be obliterated. Not even a trailhound could find them there.

In the afternoon, they heard the roar of shotguns as hunters from White Bead sought quail in a nearby field of maize stalks. After the hunters left, the coyotes came down off the hill to investigate the hunted territory. This time, it was Reddy who had the good fortune to smell and pounce upon a crippled bobwhite. So sharp was his hunger that he shared very little of it with his new companion.

The famine worsened, and the drought with it. The two young coyotes separated. For two days Reddy captured nothing, although he traveled miles. He did eat a piece of white string and an old fragment of harness leather, but he got little nourishment from either. Then the young female rejoined him and together they explored the country for food, finding none.

On Saturday, the pickups invaded. Hound packs thronged the Wilderness. All day, the two coyotes lay in hiding near the hilltop, watching them go past.

In mid-afternoon, the odor of gasoline fumes again alerted them. The orange pickup appeared, bumping slowly over the wasteland. Dietz's California pack was in the dog box and Dietz's resolute face was clenched over the steering wheel, his black eyes peering all about.

Reddy flattened himself behind the knoll, growling under his breath. He knew that the government professional was looking for him. He felt restless and nervous and tormented. Never had he been hunted as persistently as this man was hunting him now. Every time he put a foot down, he had to watch where he stepped.

Each day, Dietz came to the Wilderness until it seemed that the Wilderness was this man's home, as well as his own.

At dawn, Dietz would bring his pack, their wet muzzles thrust against the screen of the dog box, and scout all morning for Reddy. In the afternoon, he would concentrate on the other coyotes, setting his traps or placing his poison pellets in areas from which other hunters had been forewarned. He knew that Reddy was too intelligent to be deceived by these devices. He was saving Reddy for his hounds.

Sometimes, carrying rifle and binoculars, he would climb to a pinnacle on the red ridge and glass the land for hours, searching for coyotes, but particularly for the coppery one whose ears he was determined to have before he concluded his campaign of extermination and returned to his California headquarters.

Another facet of his campaign also remained unfinished. Although he had slain so many Wilderness coyotes that there were barely enough left for the coursings, he had not cleared up the mystery of the lamb murders. Solving them was business, but running down Reddy was personal.

One evening just before dark, Reddy was hunting

for mice in Buck Karns' pasture. Sheep grazed peacefully all around him, and as far as Reddy was concerned, it would remain a peaceful grazing. Ever since his adventure with the strychnine, he had resolved never again to plunder these gentle, white-fleeced creatures.

And then he saw her—the yellow coyote—stalking the sheep. Like a golden missile, she hurled herself upon them and this time she cut the throats of three lambs instead of one. Bolder now, she killed for sport as well as for sustenance, Reddy saw.

Despite his own hunger, Reddy fled the scene. As he left, gliding noiselessly through the greasewood, an unfortunate thing happened. Coming around a hill on horseback, John Selman, Karns' foreman, saw and recognized him. When, on the following morning, Selman found the carcasses of the lambs, he remembered.

Buck Karns, goaded by the wave of killings that not even Dietz had solved, acted with characteristic impulsiveness. Driving to Huckel, the county seat, he called on the editor of the *Messenger,* and giving his personal check, posted a $300 reward for the capture, dead or alive, of Reddy the coyote.

After that, the struggle for life became deadlier than ever for Reddy. Not only was he harassed increasingly by hunters seeking the reward, but the snows kept coming and the numbing cold remained. The young female hunted with him constantly now and ran with him and lived with him, too.

But they lived dangerously. The Wilderness, the region where he wanted to rear his family, was now a place of terror and of death. Dietz had done his grim job well. No segment of the land had escaped his stern patrol.

When Reddy entered a tract of sand and Indian grass where back in October he had occasionally flushed cottontails, a young coyote stared at him with pleading eyes, one hind foot snagged in a trap.

When Reddy took his companion to the old haunt where he had been born, the badger hole beneath the wild plum clump, they found the body of Buff, a bullet through his belly. Dietz's tracks and scent were everywhere. Studying the maze of tracks, Reddy saw what had happened.

Dietz, in his pickup, had flushed the three pups that Buff was feeding at such labor. When they had fled around the small hill, Dietz had run to its summit, knowing that he would have several open shots at them.

A coyote ran out of the arroyo at the bottom of the hill. Dietz shot it. But when he went to it, he saw that instead of a young one, he had slain the father who had not hesitated to risk his life trying to divert attention away from his family.

Pointing his nose at the moon, Reddy howled his grief. The female's voice pealed out piercingly beside him as she shared his woe.

Food continued so difficult to find that Reddy was

almost driven to watching the soaring of the turkey buzzards whose philosophy of "what matters who kills the game when we can all eat it?" many coyotes shared. But first he tried something else.

Over the thin skim of snow that coated the buffalo grass, he led his companion to the Peter Zook farm. In the northeast corner of the river pasture a tall straight-backed man without a gun was pouring cotton-seed cake into long feeding troughs for his cattle.

Bundled warmly against the cold, the man had wrapped a gray muffler around his ears, drawn storm mittens on his hands, and had draped his lank body in a khaki greatcoat, supplemented by a cape around the shoulders. Reddy did not recognize him until he moved down wind and got a noseful of the man's scent.

Of all the scents Reddy had filed away in the many drawers of his orderly mind, he remembered with the most assurance those of Peter Zook and his daughter Susy. Theirs were scents of human beings who had never tried to hurt him, scents that in spite of his shyness and inborn fear he thought he could trust.

After Peter Zook finished the feeding and rode off on the same buckskin horse that Reddy had so often seen him riding during his puppyhood at the Zook farm, Reddy trotted to the cattle troughs where the bovines were noisily crushing the tan pellets between their jaws.

Some of the food had fallen to the ground. Moving fearlessly among the cattle, Reddy sniffed the fallen pellets.

They smelled appetizing. There was no scent of any poison that he knew. The cattle were eating them. They had been poured into the troughs by Zook.

Reddy munched one, tentatively, and liked it. He stood warily, ready to vomit it if the pains and nausea came. They did not.

Turning to where his companion was hidden in the sandlove grass, he barked once, sharply, and she ran lightly to his side.

They ate like starved jackals. Quickly exhausting the meagre supply on the ground, the coyotes waited until the cattle had finished, then leaped into the feeding troughs, scouring them. The high-protein food imparted strength and vigor and took the edge off their fierce appetites.

At dinner that night Peter Zook turned to his daughter. "Your coyote I think maybe I saw this afternoon. The one with the three-hundred-dollar reward on his head."

With a loud clatter, Susy dropped her fork on the floor. She stared at her father, her lips twisting with excitement. "Where did you see him?"

"In the river pasture. Almost starved, he looked. He was licking up the cottonseed cake the cattle spilled out of the feed troughs."

Rebecca clucked her tongue disapprovingly as

she handed the bottle of milk to the new baby brother lying in the cradle nearby.

"I tell you, if that scoundrel comes back on us again, he'll kill all my chickens," she said. "And nobody's sheep will be safe round here, yet."

Susy's eyes flamed. "Reddy never killed Mr. Buck Karns' sheep, Mamma's, or nobody else's sheep, either," she declared, loyally.

Peter Zook regarded her gravely. "Now stop a little while, Susy," he said. "A red coyote John Selman saw leaving the place where the lambs were killed. Your coyote is the only red one I know, yet. That looks pretty bad, don't you think?"

Susy's face clouded. Tears filmed her eyes. "Mr. John Selman never saw Reddy kill the sheep, or eat the sheep, did he?"

"No."

"Well then!" she said triumphantly, leaning down to recover the dropped fork, "he just saw Reddy running in the pasture. A coyote always has to run or he'll get killed. Everybody tries to kill him all the time."

"A smaller coyote was with him today," said Peter Zook. "Probably a female. She was shy and stayed back in the sage."

Rebecca threw up her hands. "That means they're mates. A den full of pups they'll have in April. And my chickens will have a dozen coyotes after them instead of chust one."

A roguish look crossed Peter Zook's face. "Let's see, Susy," he said, "when you owned that red coyote, you used to tell him that you were his mamma. If he has children, a grandmother that would make you, ain't so?"

Susy's eyes glowed with pleasure. She smiled all over her face. "I'm going to name his wife Gracey, after my doll that got burned," she announced.

Peter Zook's long arm reached for the lima beans. "More coyotes on this place I'd welcome yet. That government hunter has thinned them out so good that the country with rabbits is overrun. Ornery rabbits been eating my new wheat. The wheat we need to buy our staples."

The motion of his arm going past the baby's face distracted him and he dropped his bottle over the side of the cradle. It clonked loudly to the floor. Susy stooped to retrieve it for him. As she had seen her mother do, she cleaned the nipple with her napkin.

As she thrust it back into his eager mouth, placing his tiny hands around it, she listened carefully to the conversation of her parents. To Susy, coyotes were special people. And most special of them all was Reddy, her former pet.

She longed to see him. Would he still know her, she wondered?

Next day it grew warmer. Susy accompanied her father to the feeding troughs, riding behind him on the buckskin. And when the cattle spilled a few cotton-seed cake kernels on the ground, the girl picked them up, put them in her coat pocket and scattered them, pellet by pellet, along the path toward home. She also left an apple in the furrow halfway from the pasture trough to the barn.

The sky cleared that night and Reddy and Gracey used both their eyes and their noses to find the pellets in the light of the moon. And they found them, every one.

When Gracey ran onto the apple, she growled and shied away from the scent of human hands upon it. But Reddy, identifying the scent, recalled the little long-skirted girl whose fingers had rumpled the fur on top of his head. And he devoured the apple, core and all, savoring its juicy tang.

With each passing day, Reddy lost more and more of his fear of Susy and her father. Soon he would stay most of the day with Peter Zook in the field, although he cautiously kept plenty of distance between them. But Gracey, fearful and wild, stayed in the sage.

Each afternoon, Susy would spread the cotton-seed cake nearer and nearer to her home until soon Reddy went close enough to smell again the fascinating odors of the barn, the pigpen, and the chicken coop.

One morning as the sun was about to come up through the grass, Reddy stole to the top of a knoll and gazed down at the whitewashed farm buildings, luminous and rosy, where the girl had mothered him through much of his puppyhood, and at the yard that had formerly been his playground. From the stables came the sounds of cows stirring restlessly in the straw, the sleepy bleat of a lamb, the cluck of a nervous hen. But Reddy was too wise to plunder the farm upon which he lived.

Although his instincts warned him that human beings could not be trusted, his experience told him that these two could. However, he would never permit the girl or her father to come near him; he had lived too long in the wild to submit to the touch of human hands.

But when Susy walked each evening into the peach orchard and whistled to him, as she had done when he lived with her, Reddy knew what that meant. Positioning himself downwind, he would wait until dark. Then he would creep forward, approaching and backtracking and sniffing the air, until he finally came for his dinner of table scraps.

Although Gracey was reluctant to accept this strange association with humans and whined to return to the Wilderness, Reddy wisely stayed in Peter Zook's river pasture. Not only did the river throw up a barrier on the west, but the trappers, the poisoners, and the hound packs did not trespass on the Amishman's land.

With the coming of February, the days grew longer. The chocolate-colored leaves began dropping off the blackjacks and a dull green sheen glazed the buffalo grass.

At night under the stars, Reddy sang his song of courting joy, starting with a volley of yips that ran together in a doleful shriek that never failed to set off other coyotes in the area as well as excite all the house dogs within miles.

One day in mid-March, when tiny blue flowers began to hug the prairie, like confetti strewn by elves, and the wild sweet whiff of sand plum blossoms was on the air, Gracey began to investigate sheltered spots on hillsides and rock bluffs, and in hollow trees and badger holes.

To Reddy, this was mysterious behavior indeed. But when he sought to interest her in hunting, her lips would curl and a quiet growl would bubble from her throat. And he quickly saw that what she was doing was none of his affair and that he had best let her alone.

A week later, she selected a hidden spot in the cleft of a knoll three hundred yards from the windmill in Peter Zook's river pasture, the field that lay farthest from his house. She began to dig, pushing the sand out behind her until soon it formed a fan-shaped mound.

Head cocked on one side, Reddy studied her. He had noticed that when they raced, she tired quickly and that she had also reduced the range of her hunting.

Wishing to help, he walked up behind her and with his front feet attacked the mound, pushing the sand in it still farther back, whereupon she backed out of the hole and attacked him furiously. Reddy retreated and, with ears laid back, stared at her in bewilderment.

Ignoring her fatigue, she kept working until soon she was out of sight and the slap of the falling sand striking the interior walls of the hole sounded as if it came from the bowels of the earth.

At midnight, she emerged and lay resting outside the hole. Reddy came nearer, sniffing the odor of the cool, damp earth she had dug.

Hungry, he whined and tried to persuade her to hunt with him but again she snarled low in her throat and he did not push it. She seemed moody and testy and he had the idea that he was somehow involved in her strange behavior.

He hated to leave her but he grew hungrier and hungrier. At last, seeing the crimson flush of a prairie fire on the horizon, he went to it.

Scouting the terrain ahead of the crackling flames, he picked up a fleeing cottontail and ran with it back to the den.

Gracey was gone. Burying the rabbit on the spot, he trailed her three miles into the Wilderness, a place he had not visited for weeks. There he found her behind a yucca plant, digging another den.

Sinking to his haunches, Reddy studied her in puzzlement. What was wrong with the first one? To him, it seemed far safer. She worked half the night before finishing. Again she refused to let him help her.

When they returned to the den in Peter Zook's river pasture, Reddy dug up the cottontail, planning to breakfast on it. Gracey trotted up to him and boldly plucked the rabbit from his jaws. And instead of snarling at her, Reddy found himself surrendering it meekly, as if that were the proper thing to do. After that, he hunted for her as well as for himself.

Next morning, she discovered a new way to upset him. She crawled inside the den and would not come out. Distressed by her odd behavior, Reddy lay down outside, head between his paws, ears dropped dejectedly.

Just before dark, he went near Peter Zook's outbuildings, and crouching in the peach orchard, waited for Susy's whistle. Sharp as the note of a quail, it came. Among the food she left him was a red apple.

But when he carried it to Gracey and, holding it in his mouth, stuck his head into the den to give it to her, she flung herself upon him with slashing teeth and ferocious snarls. Dropping the apple, he fled ignominiously.

He hunted for himself the rest of the night. Just before dawn, he returned. Gracey was his mate and he had no intention of deserting her. Strange new forces were working on him.

Determined to investigate Gracey's welfare even

if it meant getting fanged again, he stuck his head into the hole. From its far recesses she growled at him, but not so fiercely this time. And with her, he heard a faint mewing that he did not understand.

It was then that Reddy detected the scents of the five new whelps. Eagerly, he backed out and a great excitement rippled through him. For the first time, he felt the joy of fatherhood. That the new responsibility was fraught with peril, he would soon find out.

Three nights later, when the heel of the moon dipped over the windmill in Peter Zook's river pasture, the yellow coyote hit the flocks in Cleve Henderson's field, slaying four. Cleve Henderson added one hundred dollars to the three hundred Buck Karns had already posted for the scalp of Reddy the coyote.

That excited the cupidity of somebody who had returned to the Wilderness after an absence of several months, a dirty, whiskery somebody with liquor on his breath and murder in his heart.

Always thirsty, Jud Bodkins, the wolfer, saw a chance to purchase with Reddy's scalp a store of whisky that would last for months. He would do it with his new .30–30 rifle. A rifle was quicker than traps or poison, and far less laborious, too.

In White Bead, everybody was talking about Reddy the coyote. But nobody had seen him for three weeks. Then a light clicked on in Jud Bodkins' brain.

He remembered Peter Zook purchasing the two

pups from him that morning on the creek bank. One of them had fur of a reddish hue. The Zooks liked coyotes and might be harboring this one. Greedy eyes sparkling shrewdly, the wolfer resolved to investigate.

He would take along a shovel. At this time of year, coyote mothers were suckling dens full of furry babies. He knew that Reddy would have mated by now. If he could find Reddy's children, it would mean several additional dollars in bounties.

They Can't Catch Me

Ignoring the NO TRESPASSING signs that Susy's father had posted, Jud Bodkins entered the Peter Zook farm from a direction out of sight of the house, and farthest from it, from over the river. Wading his roan, he crossed without trouble for the stream was low.

He came two hours before dawn so that he would not be seen. He brought both the rifle and the shovel. Ten minutes after he arrived, Reddy the coyote knew that he was there.

Hunting by himself near the river, Reddy heard the roan splashing through the shallows. Curious, he trailed the horse until he got close enough to scent the rider, whom he quickly identified as the wolfer. The mesh of a coyote's memory is a wonderful thing.

The shovel strapped to Jud Bodkins' saddle alarmed Reddy the most. As a pup he had heard the bite of it that morning the wolfer had dug out Smoky's brood, killing four with his ball-peen hammer. He was sure that the man intended the same fate for the new family Gracey was nursing at that moment in the den only three hundred yards away.

The odor of the gun worried Reddy less. He remembered that Jud Bodkins' rifle would reach only three hundred yards. All you had to do was stay back far enough. He thought all rifles had the same trifling range.

He found out differently when the stars began to pale an hour later.

Sniffing along the boundary of Peter Zook's alfalfa stubble, he had just pushed his face into a clump of Indian grass when it happened.

Pfwat!

The bullet tore a hole in the prairie under Reddy's nose. Leaping convulsively, the coyote was in motion almost before he heard the crack of the high-powered rifle. It was a long shot and Jud Bodkins' eye was

blurred by whisky or he might have hit the four-hundred-dollar target.

Reddy darted into a draw, preventing a second
shot. After weaving at a crouch through a stretch of
Indian grass, he came up behind a sandstone ledge and
scouted the situation.

He heard the wolfer cursing. The missed shot had
infuriated Jud Bodkins. It also reminded him of his
danger. Afraid that the rifle report might have been
heard, or that he himself might be seen, he mounted
his horse, recrossed the stream, and galloped away.

Reddy thought that the man was gone forever and
that all the danger was past.

That night, when the stars had taken over from
the last of the sunset, Reddy again heard the *kerplunk,
kerplunk, kerplunk* of a horse fording the shallows of
the river. Quickly, he circled until he got the wind
where he wanted it. Again, Jud Bodkins' scent came
floating in, thick and warm and menacing. Reddy
stiffened with fright and backed away.

This time the wolfer planned a longer stay. He
had brought not only the rifle and the shovel, but
lashed to the saddle a bed roll, a can of coffee, a twist
of liverwurst, a bottle of Old Crow and a ball-peen
hammer.

It was then that Reddy learned that his own aim
in life had changed. Previously, most of his concern

had been for himself. But now he was a father.

His lips working in a low snarl, Reddy lay down on the prairie, back legs hunched at his hips, tail spread straight out behind, staring at Jud Bodkins. This man was a threat, Reddy knew. Death was his motive—death for Gracey and the five pups.

With Reddy following but staying out of sight, Jud Bodkins rode brazenly into Peter Zook's river pasture. Lighting no fire, he took off the pack, then the saddle. He removed the bridle, hanging it on a bush. Using a picket rope, he staked out the horse in a hollow that would hide him.

Carrying his rifle and his bottle, he walked a quarter of a mile to a thicket of wild plum and sat down in it. And then a queer thing happened.

The wolfer lifted something to his lips and Reddy, hidden in the brush nearby, was amazed to hear the squeal of a wounded rabbit, a distress call so genuine that any coyote hearing it would come running to get a free meal.

But Reddy had seen it, as well as heard it, and suddenly he knew its purpose.

The contrivance Bodkins used was a predator call. For an hour, the wolfer blew it and also another that sounded like a chicken clucking in fear. But he was raising the bottle to his lips as often as he did both devices, and soon the calls began to lose their authenticity.

Cursing, the wolfer returned to camp. He decided to get a few hours' sleep then, arising before dawn, try for Reddy with his rifle and also look for dens. Pulling off his boots, he crawled into the bed roll. Soon, Reddy, hidden in the brush, began to hear a noise that sounded like one he had known in his days at Peter Zook's home, the noise of Rebecca Zook's carpet sweeper being pushed across the rug. He knew that Jud Bodkins slept and that it was time to act.

First, he barked once from deep in the sage, seeking to know for certain if the wolfer had brought Caesar or any other dog who might have crossed farther down the stream. There was no answering outcry.

Silent as a shadow, Reddy stole into the wolfer's camp and approached the roan. Smelling the coyote, the horse jumped and snorted, but the noise like the carpet sweeper continued without a break.

With his strong back teeth, Reddy sheared the picket rope in two. Discovering that he was free, the roan wandered off, munching as he moved.

Then the coyote turned his attention to Jud Bodkins' boots which were filled with the man's hated scent. After chewing one boot half in two with his scissorlike teeth, and eating the shoestring, Reddy hid the remnant in the sage. The other boot he carried to the river and buried in the sand.

Returning, he chewed the bridle into fragments. He found the liverwurst. Eyes on the snoring wolfer, he sniffed it all over, checking for poison but finding none. With great relish, he ate part of it and with a final look at the snoring wolfer, carried the rest home to Gracey whom he found hunting outside the den.

Gracey sniffed suspiciously at the liverwurst. The man's odor was still upon it. With Reddy following, she backtracked his trail to the wolfer's camp, viewing with consternation the sleeping enemy who had established himself so near to her darlings.

In a flash, Gracey made up her mind. Back to the den she trotted with Reddy at her heels. She ducked inside the den. She came out, holding in her mouth a pup by the scruff of the neck. It was a tiny cinnamon-furred male.

Fascinated at his first sight of one of his children, even in the moonlight, Reddy whined eagerly and pressed closer to sniff his son. But Gracey did not linger to give him a second look or a second smell. Breaking into a run, she set off for the Wilderness.

Reddy knew where his duty lay. Crawling into the den, he thrust his nose into the nest of babies, licking them. They lifted their tiny paws and chewed at the thick fur around his neck.

Carefully grasping one of them by the back of the neck, he backed out and began trailing Gracey to the alternate den she had dug behind the yucca in the Wilderness. It was a three-mile trip but he bore it uncomplainingly. She had always wanted to den there, he knew. He followed her with great caution. The Wilderness was out of bounds to him now.

The whole country was looking for him there. But he saw the wisdom of the transfer and worked nearly all night helping her move the whelps, a labor involving thirty miles of travel. Jud Bodkins slept on and on.

Next morning, Peter Zook on the buckskin, hunting for another lost cow, found Jud Bodkins walking barefoot in his river pasture. The wolfer was carrying a .30–.30 rifle.

Jud Bodkins stared angrily at Peter Zook. "You seen anything of a roan hawse?" he demanded. He sounded as if he suspected the Amishman of stealing the animal.

Reining in, Peter Zook puckered his brows in concentrated thought. "What for in my pasture are you doing with a gun?" he asked mildly. He looked behind the wolfer. The man's trail, a dark smear across the dew-soaked buffalo grass, was plain.

Leaving Jud standing in the pasture, Peter Zook touched his heels to the buckskin's flanks. Following the wolfer's wet trail across the prairie, he came upon the bed roll, the saddle, the shovel, the severed picket rope, and the empty whiskey bottle.

Then he rode back to the wolfer. Jud Bodkins stood, surly and defiant, holding the rifle.

Peter Zook said gently, "A man's printed signs you pay no attention to, ain't so?"

The wolfer leered at him as if the question were an impertinence that no man as queer and foreign looking as this one should ask him under any circumstances.

"I ain't got no time to argue with you about a bunch of damn pasteboard," he replied, "I'll argue that out with the owner of this property."

"I'm the owner," said Peter Zook, "and I'm entitled to an answer to my question."

"You don't own nothin' an' you ain't gettin' no answer from me," Jud Bodkins sneered. He moved a step closer, shifting the rifle to both hands and raising the barrel.

"Git down off thet hawse," he commanded. "I'm gonna borrow him. I'll bring him back soon as I find mine." From the sage, Reddy the coyote watched with curiosity this confrontation between the man he feared the most and the only man he trusted.

For the second time in his life, Peter Zook felt his temper ruffling, as a gust of wind ruffles the surface of a prairie pond. How well he remembered the first time.

Jacob Yoder, the Amish bishop, had forbidden him to keep the tractor. Every time Peter saw the bishop's boxlike buggy approaching from a distance, Peter had hitched a horse to the tractor and left them standing in the yard, with the horse looking back curiously over his shoulder at the vehicle to which he was attached.

Tiring of this subterfuge, Peter used his tractor openly whereupon the bishop banned him from the church. And when the bishop drove up again and Peter knew he was facing further spiritual shunning and every day avoidance by his family and his friends, he lost control. Grasping the cleric by his seven-inch beard, he towed him off the premises. Still angry, Peter sold his Pennsylvania farm and started one in western Oklahoma. And now he was up against this bullying wolfer.

As Peter loosened his outside foot in the stirrup, he struggled with his Mennonite tradition of non-violence. Slowly, he swung his right leg over the back of his saddle and dismounted. Now both his feet were on the ground. His right hand lingered lightly on the saddle.

And then Peter lost the struggle. Jud Bodkins stepped forward, reaching for the bridle reins.

Peter Zook's right fist, traveling only a foot, sent with the shift of the body from right to left behind it, nailed Jud Bodkins squarely on his whiskered jaw, a tooth-rattling blow. To Peter's astonishment, the wolfer went down and his rifle flew harmlessly out of his hand.

With the crack of the punch, Reddy the coyote flattened himself in the sage, his hair standing on end. He was prepared to flee, if necessary.

It was not necessary. What followed pleased Reddy if for no other reason than it resulted in the

departure of Jud Bodkins. Peter Zook picked up the rifle and ejected the shells. The wolfer's manner changed from snarling bully to cowering recreant.

Peter Zook put Jud Bodkins on the buckskin. Riding behind him, he delivered him and his rifle to the sheriff in the courthouse at Huckel. Invited to file trespassing charges, he waved off the county attorney.

"Wait, once." he said. "That's not my religion. We Amish believe that love is the all of life. This man is a *schussel,* but he's also a child of God—same as you and me—and I was wrong to strike him. I'm not going to file on him and hurt him again."

And that was the end of that.

But it wasn't the end of trouble for Reddy the coyote. Early the following morning, the prairie was dim with a predawn haze and there was fog in the low places. Reddy's belly was full.

On the White Bead highway, he had found the warm body of a fat possum that had been run over by an automobile. Planning to regurgitate it later for the pups and Gracey, Reddy ate most of the possum and was carrying the rest of it to the Wilderness den. Gracey was coming to meet him, two hundred yards away.

Reddy's first sight of the orange pickup came so abruptly that there was time only for a quick bark to warn Gracey. The pickup was parked behind a small rise one hundred yards downwind in a place where neither of them could smell it.

Behind it, several other pickups stood in a dark and silent line as support to Jack Dietz. This was Dietz's final hunt before returning next day to California. His pack was to be given the honor of running down Reddy, if the coyote could be flushed.

Somebody else, a tall, oldish man with long gray sideburns, had come to see the chase and to make an on-the-spot check of Dietz's campaign to stop the lamb killing. He was Hank Bailey, chief of the government's Predator Control division. He had flown to the Wilderness country. J. C. Clack, the ranger, had driven to the Amarillo airport to bring him. The newcomer was a guest at the Clack home. Dietz had joined them there for dinner the night before.

The farmers did not know it then, but Bailey had an announcement to make that would profoundly interest them. But there would be no opportunity until after the hunt.

At last, Dietz knew where to look for Reddy, but he had kept this information to himself. At the courthouse in Huckel, he had been told by the sheriff that Jud Bodkins had nearly missed shooting the red coyote in Peter Zook's river pasture.

Reddy crouched in the greasewood. At last, his showdown race with Dietz and his pack had come. Caught with a bulging belly, Reddy felt as foolish as a six-month-old pup who had stepped into a trap with both front feet.

Dietz yanked the wire of his dog box. Through the door leaped the pack in a moving ribbon that broke and frayed into individual hounds. And Gracey was directly in their path.

A coyote husband is a loving beast, even with his stomach full of possum.

Reddy wound up his tail. Electrifying himself into instant action, he flashed between Gracey and the Blue Gyp. He barely made it. And the effort it required discouraged him profoundly. He felt as if his stomach was full of stones.

"There he is! There's the red one!" he heard Dietz yell, "Zap him! Zap him!" The sun, peeking over the horizon, dappled the wet shortgrass with exaggerated shadows. Over this the orange pickup roared in pursuit.

To Reddy's left, a fog bank, cool and milk white, lay over the river plain. With all the speed in his legs, Reddy ran toward it.

He needed that fog. A plan, bold and desperate, formed in his mind as he ran, a plan that might buy him a little time. Behind him, he could hear the Blue Gyp, silent except for little half-suppressed yelps of excitement, tailing him closely. He knew that in a straight dash, carrying all that breakfast, he would never reach the fog ahead of her.

Faking to go left, he suddenly dug his claws into the wet grass and cut right. Behind him, he heard the hounds squealing, grunting, and scratching with their toenails as they lost momentum trying to turn with him.

That maneuver won him thirty yards and he plunged from sight into the pearl-gray mist, feeling as if he had vaulted into another world.

Pulling up, he vomited all the possum meat. Instantly, he felt better. But the fog, tinted in pink, lilac, and pale yellow, had begun to lift. Through it, the sun appeared as a silver disk.

Dietz's angry shouts, scolding his dogs and summoning the Walker, cut through the gloom close to him. In a clear spot off to the right, Reddy saw through light growing more golden by the moment the Blue Gyp bounding up and down in futile sky hops as she tried to spot him in the mist.

Reddy had learned that staghounds can scent as well as see. From deep in the fog bank, the sound of their snuffling came closer and closer. He knew that in another five seconds they would have him.

Suddenly the wind parted the fog, revealing long vistas of the prairie. Recess was over and the chase had convened again.

Staying in the shreds of mist as long as possible, he ran two hundred yards before Dietz saw him, and mashing his hand down on the pickup horn, pointed him out to the pack.

Reddy ran lightly and thoughtfully, his short legs twinkling over the curly buffalo grass. He welcomed this race with Dietz's hounds, led by the blue reject.

They were the best by far in the Wilderness. But Reddy knew that he could run, too.

He ran with his heart as well as with his legs. The things that made him formidable were in him all the time: his determination, his pride, and his poise. It was something he had got from his mother and his father, and from growing up and surviving in this wild habitat that threw out so many tough challenges.

He ran with great confidence. His heart seemed to be singing a bold little tune, a tune of daring, and defiance, and exultation. His flitting feet seemed to tap out the refrain. *They can't catch me, they can't catch me, they can't catch me.*

Like a wisp of red vapor, Reddy drifted along a wash. His blood was pumping fast. The bite of the morning air was on his face and in his eyes. The variety of the course, its ever-changing footing, the alternation of its gentle rises and receding hollows, and winding around its gypsum-veined buttes presented no problem. It was his kind of terrain and he felt a oneness with it.

Casting a look over his shoulder, he saw the California hounds striding like machines, their lithe bodies bending to the work. Behind them hurried the orange pickup, straddling the ditches, jumping the gullies, skirting the high centers. For the present he would have to run an open trail where the hounds could see him all the time and Dietz would not be bothered with tracking.

He felt as if he was running Dietz instead of his pack of trained killers. But they all had to run where he took them. So why not take them where it was difficult?

A rifle shot cut the air over his head. Although Reddy did not know it, Dietz was not trying to hit him. Seeing that his pack had failed to score the sensational gains he wanted, he hoped to fluster the coyote into making some mistake that would cost him yardage.

Instead, it galvanized Reddy into a super effort. He really had not wanted to hunt cover anyhow; to run them into the earth was his dearest wish. The hunt had emerged into the clear, in full view of the pickups that followed, their shortwave radios babbling with excitement.

Whirling his tail in a half circle, the coyote bent his line to the left, along the ridge, and reached his full pace.

The yucca, the tamarisk, and the mesquite rippled backward as he took a downward grade with the bursting rush of an antelope buck. Dietz would see a brand of running he had never seen before.

Through a grove of shinnery mottled with dark shadows, around a prairie dog town whose sleepy occupants sat in the doors of their homes gawking with awe, past a buffalo wallow where the killdeers called plaintively, "Oh dear! Oh dear! Oh dear!" swept the chase. So swift was Reddy's flight that his coat, like an artist's brush, laid a burnt sienna streak against the green of the ridge.

When Reddy flung a look over his shoulder, he was troubled to find that despite his sprint, the distance between him and the Blue Gyp had lessened to a hundred and twenty-five yards.

Bent over, she was coming in long leaps, skimming the prairie pompously, as if she spurned and despised it. Close behind her, profiled against the sky, the grizzled staghounds swung along powerfully, never uttering a sound and never for a moment taking their fierce stare off Reddy.

The coyote did not understand. Pride and courage still flowed hotly in him, although he was beginning to feel pressure from the pace.

He responded by pouring out the last of his speed in a final desperate effort. But he could not long maintain it. When he chanced another rearward look, his margin over the Blue Gyp and the staghounds had shrunk to seventy-five yards.

His mother had been right. Straightaway speed was a treacherous delusion. A coyote's greatest heritage is his intelligence, and he must never forget it. These formidable beasts owned by Dietz were running him off his feet. He was going to be overtaken. And once he was, they would kill him faster than fire would scorch a feather.

The Haven

    Desperate, he tried strategy. He was still the one who decided where the race would go. He tried to concentrate, to detach himself from things, to think ahead.

    He ran to the locality where he had tricked Dietz's hounds, by starting left down the arroyo, then cutting right to the cottonwood tree. This time there was no horn toot from the orange pickup, and he knew that Dietz, refusing to take the cut-across bait, was keeping the pack right on him.

Bearing to the right, Reddy ran for the slanting cottonwood. But when he sought to run up its trunk, leap into its foliage and hide, a wildcat, cradling in his paws a dead mouse, snarled at him from the main bough. And next time he looked back, he could scarcely believe his eyes. The Blue Gyp was only forty yards behind.

Reddy tried for Sand Creek, only to find it dry. Behind him, he heard for the first time the crisp, continuing patter of the Blue Gyp's feet and her fierce panting and eager squealing as she pressed him closer and closer. Then they had him out on the open plain.

From the sky over his head, he heard something else, the loud hum of a motor.

Jerking his head upward, Reddy expected to see the orange pickup attacking him from the heavens. Instead, he saw a gigantic yellow bird with wings that never flapped. Cruising as low as a hungry hawk, it outran him easily, waggling its wings as it passed over him. Then it banked and circled.

Unknown to Reddy, the small airplane was directing the hunt by shortwave radio. Its pilot, who had an excellent view of the coyote, kept in constant communication with Dietz's orange truck and all the other pickups in the chase.

"Your dogs are gainin', Dietz!" the shortwave relayed the pilot's excited chatter. "He's gettin' awful tired. Now he's runnin' through Grandma Boston's alfalfa but there's no place there to hide. You've got him, Dietz! You've got him!"

Again Reddy heard above him the drone of the motor and the squeaking of its shortwave radio. This time, its moving shadow darkened the prairie as it swept over him. Terrified, he tried to dodge it. Again it outran him, waggling its wings derisively and disappearing.

The chase flowed past the Clack farm where the ranger's wife was on her way to the poultry lot carrying a pan of scratch. It careened along the White Bead highway where a family riding leisurely in an old sedan stared in wonder. It swirled in front of Charley Huff's place where Grandpa Huff was hoeing in the garden. And Reddy was gasping, and his bottle-shaped tail drooped with exhaustion.

But his mind was still functioning alertly. He thought of the only break in the land's flatness, the trench in the gully behind the washed-out dam in Charley Huff's pasture. He would take them across that trench. He knew every root and wrinkle of the ground there.

Veering, Reddy headed for the dam festooned with willows. He slowed, and with a single bound that took a severe toll of his remaining strength, leaped into the trench and scrambled up the embankment beyond

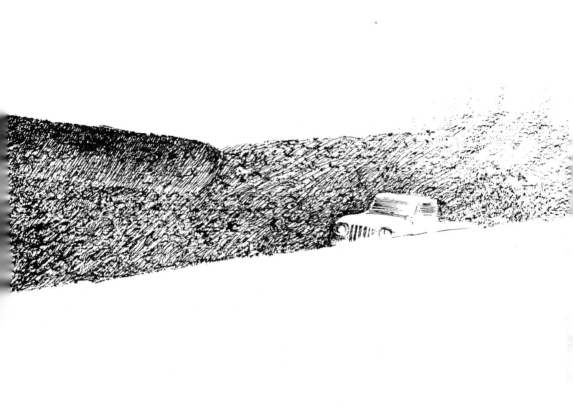

it. The hounds, crazed by the excitement of the chase
and the nearness of the victim, never saw the trench.
They rashly tried to follow at full speed.

With sickening thuds, the leaders struck the far
edge of the trench and were flipped on their backs. The
impact was shattering. The Blue Gyp and two of the
staghounds lay on their sides. For an instant, their long
legs flailed the air. Then they grew quiet and inert.

Behind him, Reddy heard the orange pickup,
brakes squeaking, slide to a stop. Dietz yanked the
wire to another rear compartment, releasing Jomo, the
killer.

The big crossbred Irish and Russian wolfhound
shouldered through the opening and leaped out. Set-
tling into a pounding stride, he joined the five remaining staghounds after Reddy. Fresh, he quickly drew up
with them.

Reddy, tired and spent, made himself keep going
on legs that had lost all feeling. He had gained back
twenty yards over the trench but all it brought him was
room in which to zigzag weakly as the sinister gray
shapes closed on him again.

For a moment, he knew how lonely and terrified
every coyote feels just before it is pulled down and
ripped open—Skeezix, the Texas coyote, the Old One.
And all the grandparents and great-grandparents on
both sides of his family. But the will to live still burned
brightly within him.

Ahead, the path ended suddenly in a barley field buffered by a coyote-proof sheep fence, an eight-foot barrier of net wire with an apron on the ground. Calling on his last flicker of energy, Reddy climbed that fence like a cat and jumped down beyond it. But Dietz, behind him, slid the pickup's wheels, sprang out, and hazed his dogs around it.

Fagged, Reddy ran into a culvert, then out of it. He ran into a second culvert and out the other end of it. Dietz, sprinting and hallowing, kept the dogs after him. And Reddy knew that his time was up.

Ahead of him, the white outbuildings of the Zook farm sprawled in the morning sunshine. The coyote glided toward them like a weary shadow. His brush dragged and his tongue was swollen and black. He felt as if the pads had been run off his feet.

In the barn lot, Susy Zook saw him coming. At his flanks raced two staghounds. Instinctively they allowed the space between them to widen, so one could take him by the hind leg and the other by the throat. Red-eyed, riled and savage, Jomo ran just behind them, dropping his shoulders for the kill.

Susy recognized the coyote. Her eyes widened at the sight of him.

"Red-deeeeeeeeee!" she shrieked, her voice striking echoes off the river bluffs. Dropping to one knee, she held out both arms.

The coyote saw the long skirt and black poke

bonnet of his former mistress. The discovery gave him an extra spark of vitality.

Reaching into the very bottom of his reservoir of spirit and valor, he accelerated, heading straight for Susy. His toenails clicked across the concrete spillway. Sobbing for breath, he plunged into the girl's waiting arms.

The impact of his body drove her back, but holding him on one shoulder, she ran into the barn and slammed the door. Leaping from her arms, Reddy saw the bundles of baled prairie hay stacked high in the connecting shed. While he climbed them and lay panting out of sight on top, Susy latched the door.

And turning, she thought with breathless pleasure of the coyote she had mothered and fed, lost and cried over, and now had recovered again.

Outside, the Zook dogs were fighting with Dietz's dogs. The yard filled with pickups of every hue. The pilot of the small yellow plane expertly set it down in a nearby pasture.

Rebecca Zook, her middle-parted hair covered with the white prayer cap, was shining pots and pans in the kitchen. Her husband, mending harness, had come to the house for a thick needle.

"Peter," she called, "Go look the window out and see who is coming the yard in."

Dietz drove back to the trench near Charley

Huff's dam where three of his hounds lay on the grass, two dead with broken necks. The Blue Gyp, he saw, had fractured both front feet. With luck, she could hunt next season.

When Wolf Thompson drove up in his old gray pickup and got out, Dietz was standing over one of his dead staghounds.

"Is he dead?" asked Wolf Thompson.

Dietz glared at him. "He's gettin' cold and stiff. He's stopped breathin'." He kicked the body with one foot. "He don't move when I kick him. Wouldn't you call that dead?"

Wolf Thompson grinned crookedly. "Kinda puts you out of the coyote huntin' business, don't it, captain?" he said.

Dietz did not answer. Tenderly, he picked up the Blue Gyp and placed her in the front seat of the orange pickup. Wolf Thompson helped him load the dead staghounds in the rear.

Dietz drove the short distance to Peter Zook's farm. There, the other farmers and ranchers milled angrily in the barn lot. They looked like vigilantes after an outlaw.

Dietz got out. Black eyes gleaming, he walked among them.

"Where's the coyote?" he asked.

Lige Lancaster nodded toward the barn door

from which Susy Zook emerged, a finger in her mouth. She quickly shut the door behind her and turned to stare fearfully at the visitors.

"Who owns this place?" demanded Dietz.

Peter Zook moved in front of him, next to Susy, blocking the barn door. "I do," he replied, courteously.

Dietz glared at him. "I want your permission to go in there and shoot that coyote." Although his voice was edged with hostility, he was observing the correct legal procedure. He had to obtain permission.

Peter Zook shook his head. "I'm sorry, mister, but I won't permit that. This coyote is my daughter's pet. She feeds it, and likes it, yet. You saw it jump into her arms just now ahead of those hounds."

"He wouldn't a been ahead of 'em if the Blue Gyp hadn't lamed herself on that ditch back there," said Frank Thorne. Wrathful and black mustached, he had pushed into the front rank of men.

"I don't know about thet!" said little Wolf Thompson, swaggering fearlessly forward. "Anything runnin' second in a race has the advantage. It can see the leader in front all the time. When the leader changes course, the one behind can cut across an' gain ground. It knows when to make its move. It's easier to foller pace than to make it."

Cleve Henderson pushed forward, eyes fixed on Peter Zook with cold fury. "You're the only farmer in this whole country who has posted his land against coyote hunters," he said, hotly.

Peter Zook ignored him. He knew that Henderson had suffered losses to coyote depredators. Most of the men, he saw, were excited and wrathful and on the verge of taking precipitate action. A few, like Charley Huff and Milo Briggs, hung back shamefaced and would not look him in the eye.

"Feed a coyote and it'll kill all your chickens," sneered Tige Ralston. Under his red sweater, his beefy shoulders were hunched aggressively, as if he was about to lead the dash into the barn.

Peter Zook faced him. "This girl of mine has been feeding this one for weeks and he hasn't a chicken bothered yet," he said, patiently. "Of course, he may some time if he's starving. But what's a chicken or two compared to all the good he does?"

Susy, cowering near her father's side, groped for his big hand, found it, clutched it tightly. She sensed the antagonism of the group and gloried in her father's courage.

Dietz's black eyes bored into Peter Zook's. "I've got the right—and I think you know it—to come onto privately owned land after a varmint that's injurious to agriculture or to stock."

"Yes. You certainly have, Mr. Dietz," acknowledged Peter Zook, "But the law, I think, says that first you have to cooperate with the owner. I would not co-operate with you on that. A court order you can get from the federal judge at Oklahoma City, but a hearing I can demand. And I think I could show that ninety percent of all coyotes are good citizens and deserve to live."

Unseen by most, the pilot of the small yellow plane and his older companion, the tall man with the long gray sideburns, had walked up and were listening.

The way Peter Zook stood showed that he was sure of his ground here. "Coyotes, you say, are hurting the crops. I'm saying that when you kill off coyotes, you let things like mice, rats, moles, and ground squirrels have the crops. If you have time, I will take you to my field right now and show you where the gophers are working in my alfalfa."

Peter Zook shifted his feet resolutely. His voice was quiet but earnest. "A pair of gophers will nip the sprouts of an eighth of an acre in one season. The jack-rabbits my range grass are eating. One jackrabbit will eat as much in a day as a horse. Coyotes keep down all these pests. One of my own dogs I'd as soon shoot as I would a coyote."

Tige Ralston sneered. "I'll shoot a coyote any time I can get him in my sights. They're cowardly things."

"A coyote is the guttiest animal I know, yet," said Peter Zook. "Only twenty-five to thirty pounds he weighs but he will take on half a dozen dogs, all of them bigger than he is. He has got to be gutty to stay alive. Open season it always is on coyotes. Twelve months of every year we're after him."

"Yeah," broke in Wolf Thompson. "An' we rob his dens, and kill his pups. States and counties pay bounties on him. An' stock associations hire professionals to destroy him." He looked straight at Dietz.

"I know it's fun to hunt coyotes with dogs," admitted Peter Zook, "I, too, do it. I haven't caught one yet but it's fun. It's sport."

"Yeah," echoed Wolf Thompson, "Sport fer ever' one but the coyote. Today we had somethin' like twenty men, forty dogs, eight pickups, an' an airyoplane all after this red coyote. An' he beat us all. If a coyote loses the race, he loses his life. If we lose, all it costs us is a buck's worth of gasoline and our dogs' breath."

"He gets no game sanctuary. . . ." continued Peter Zook.

"An' needs none," seconded Wolf Thompson. "He kin take care of hisself. He's too smart fer us. The worst thing he's done is refuse to let us kill him off."

Tige Ralston laughed in Wolf Thompson's face. It was a nasty laugh with promise of a fight in it. "If he's as noble as all that, how come he's killin' sheep?" he said.

His voice had a brittle quality that denoted a

vanishing patience. "There's a four-hundred-dollar reward on the coyote in thet barn. He's a lamb killer. An'
I say let's go in and get him!"

Afraid for her father, Susy felt herself shrinking
into a shivering knot. Peter Zook pushed her gently to
one side.

"Go the house into, Susy, and help Mamma redd up
the rooms," he said. But he was not looking at her. He
had never taken his eyes off Tige Ralston.

"Wait a minute, men," an authoritative voice bit
through the tumult. The tall, oldish man with the long
gray sideburns who had come from the airplane walked
forward and turned, facing the crowd. On the lapel of
his coat, a badge glinted in the sunshine.

J. C. Clack, the ranger, stepped forward with him.
"Men," he said, "this is Hank Bailey, chief of the government's Predator Control division. He watched this
morning's hunt from the air in Arch Alexander's Piper
Cub. He came to see for himself how thorough a job
Jack Dietz has done controlling coyotes in this locality."

The new man looked around. There was a
strength and authority about him that impressed everybody. "Mr. Dietz has also done something else that he's
been too modest to tell you about," he said. "Nearly all
the sheep killing anywhere is done by one individual
coyote. Last night, Jack got your sheep killer."

Pausing, he let his eyes sweep them again, enjoying the surprise in their faces. "She was a yellow female. He got her with a long rifle shot on George Laney's ranch. Spotted her with his field glass slipping along a terrace. Saw her kill the sheep and start to eat it." He looked at Dietz who ducked his head and toed the earth bashfully.

That surprising announcement eased the tension. From the boxes in the pickups, the hounds stood with lifted ears, listening gravely.

Hank Bailey turned to Peter Zook. "I like your defense of this particular coyote," he said, "and for your daughter's sake, I'm glad he came clean. The economic status of a coyote is often a question of locality. You like him on your land and with good reason. But Mr. Karns, Mr. Thorne, Mr. Laney, and Mr. Henderson don't like him on theirs and they have good reasons, too. Expensive reasons."

He faced the others again. "I want to make it plain that the Predator Control division isn't trying to exterminate the coyote. All we're trying to do is control him on sheep, goat, and cattle ranges. And on wildlife management and restoration areas. We don't stay in one place forever. When we get the real killer, we move on. And now we're ready to move on here."

He took off his big gray hat, looked at it thoughtfully, put it on again. "Hounds aren't an official part of our control machinery, but hounds kill lots of coyotes. And hounds are emotional objects. I know that all you gentlemen are as fond of your hounds as this young lady"—he nodded toward Susy—"is of her coyote. We've had good sport here this morning. I just saw the finest coyote chase I've ever seen in my life. Thank you very much."

His remarks, calm and reasonable, eliminated all the emotion. Things gentled down. The yard soon emptied of men, dogs, and pickups.

Afterward, Susy did not go back into the barn to look for Reddy. She was remembering her grandmother's old proverb. "You must never watch a friend out of sight, or you will never see him again."

Susy wanted to see Reddy again, and again, and again. But now that he was grown, she would let him select the time.

Reddy would not have been in the barn even if she had gone back to it. During the argument in the barn lot, he had leaped through a rear window and run to the den in Peter Zook's river pasture.

To his surprise, someone was there ahead of him, the cold wind rippling her fur. It was Gracey with a pup in her mouth.

And Reddy laughed as coyotes laugh, with his yellow slanted eyes and his lolling pink tongue.

Gracey was moving back.

And that's how Reddy the coyote grew so wise in the ways of the Wilderness that he overcame the perils of extinction, learned to match wits with the hunters, the trappers, and the poisoners, and won for his family and his species a promise of future happiness in the midst of a hostile world.

Author's Note

Three veteran coyote hunters, Clarence Tignor, Sr., of Sweetwater, Oklahoma; Lewis "Cat" Harmon of Norman, Oklahoma; and the late George Eubanks of Fairview, Oklahoma, gave valuable aid and counsel in personal interviews to the research of this story.

Because I wanted the authentic flavor of a coyote hunt with hounds, I drove to Sweetwater, and as Mr. Tignor's guest, observed one on the Texas-Oklahoma line, midway between Oklahoma City and Amarillo, Texas. It was a memorable experience.

Mr. Eubanks kindly read the story in manuscript. So did an English class at Fairview, Oklahoma, high school.

All the human characters in the story are ficticious, but most of the coyotes and hounds are not and this is no coincidence.

For assistance in researching the tale's Amish phase, my informants were three Mennonite students at the University of Oklahoma, Connie Heinrichs, Kristina Ediger, and Pat Unruh, all living near Enid, Oklahoma; Mrs. Frances Dunham of Norman, Oklahoma; Dennis Reimer of Weatherford, Oklahoma; Leonard Johnson of Corn, Oklahoma; D. J. Gerbrandt of Norman, Oklahoma, a Canadian-born Mennonite who is coordinator in special education for the State of Oklahoma Department of Education, and Mrs. Gerbrandt. Mrs. Irene Bartel of Weatherford and Miss Heinrichs aided with the Mennonite speech and dialect.

Others who helped were Bill Porter of Norman, sheriff of Cleveland County; Preston Trimble of Norman, district attorney; Reginald Gaston of Norman, legal intern; Walter Hansmeyer and O. C. Boyd, farmers living near Norman; Ted Reynolds, pastor of the Maude Reynolds Indian Mission east of Norman, and Leroy White who lives in the same locality. Mrs. Suzanne Kee of Moore, Oklahoma, typed the manuscript.

I am indebted, also, to the University of Oklahoma library of which Dr. James K. Zink is director, and to Mrs. Mary Esther Saxon, assistant professor of bibliography and fourth floor reference librarian, for permitting me to research the book there, and use a faculty study.

HAROLD KEITH

University of Oklahoma,
June 1, 1973

ABOUT THE AUTHOR

Harold Keith grew up in a small town in Oklahoma where books and outdoor life were the most popular sources of entertainment. When he wasn't reading every book he could get his hands on, he went fishing, camping, swimming, or, in the winter, ice-skating. His upbringing is reflected in his writing, which is strong and vigorous, with a marked feeling for the outdoors.

His book *Rifles for Watie* won the Newbery Medal in 1958, an award given for literary excellence. His other fine books include *Sports and Games, Brief Garland,* and *Komantcia.*

For many years Harold Keith was director of the Sports Information Center at the University of Oklahoma, but he has retired from this position and is now a full-time writer. Mr. Keith lives in Norman, Oklahoma.

ABOUT THE ARTIST

John Schoenherr received his B.F.A. from Pratt Institute and continued his education with the Art Students League of New York. He has been the recipient of nine citations from the Society of Illustrators, and the World Science Fiction Award. Mr. Schoenherr's work has also been seen in such publications as *Reader's Digest, Audubon,* and *Animal Kingdom.* He has traveled extensively throughout the United States, Canada, and Iran. He now lives with his wife and two daughters in Stockton, New Jersey.